She froze on tː
hitched in her

She must have turned ashen, though heat was surging through her veins. Zak Acosta, looking grimmer and tougher than she remembered, was standing in the doorway.

"Zak!"

"Jess..."

Those eyes...that voice...that powerful, compelling presence. His deep, sonorous voice with its seductive Spanish sibilance rolled across her senses like black velvet, brushed lightly yet so effectively across every sensitive zone she had. His eyes were black pools of experience, while his mouth was a straight, hard line. There was nothing soft or yielding about Zak Acosta—there never had been, she remembered.

Susan Stephens

ONE SCANDALOUS
CHRISTMAS EVE

HARLEQUIN®
PRESENTS®

ISBN-13: 978-1-335-14896-4

One Scandalous Christmas Eve

Copyright © 2020 by Susan Stephens

Harlequin Enterprises ULC
22 Adelaide St. West, 40th Floor
Toronto, Ontario M5H 4E3, Canada
www.Harlequin.com

Printed in U.S.A.

Susan Stephens was a professional singer before meeting her husband on the Mediterranean island of Malta. In true Harlequin style, they met on Monday, became engaged on Friday and married three months later. Susan enjoys entertaining, travel and going to the theater. To relax she reads, cooks and plays the piano, and when she's had enough of relaxing, she throws herself off mountains on skis or gallops through the countryside singing loudly.

Books by Susan Stephens

Harlequin Presents

The Sicilian's Defiant Virgin
Pregnant by the Desert King
The Greek's Virgin Temptation
Snowbound with His Forbidden Innocent

One Night With Consequences

A Night of Royal Consequences
The Sheikh's Shock Child

Passion in Paradise

A Scandalous Midnight in Madrid
A Bride Fit for a Prince?

Secret Heirs of Billionaires

The Secret Kept from the Greek

Visit the Author Profile page
at Harlequin.com for more titles.

For Pippa Roscoe, Mother of Wolves, amazing author of Harlequin Presents books and whipper-upper of enthusiasm for more Acostas. If we hadn't been chatting over tapas in a Spanish restaurant called Lobos (Wolves), Team Lobos might never have taken to the saddle.

Thank you to all involved for bringing back the dangerous glamour of the Acosta clan!

CHAPTER ONE

THE SHADOW OF a helicopter briefly dimmed the sunshine of a crisp November day. Jess Slatehome's breath hitched. The logo on the side, a shield of gold on a ground of black, stated boldly, Acosta España.

The Acostas were *back*!

It had been a long ten years since Jess had last met up with the Spanish Acosta family—four handsome brothers with an elegant sister at home—when they had come to trial some ponies on her family farm in Yorkshire.

When she had kissed one of them.

Closing her eyes briefly on that embarrassing thought, Jess knew she had to focus on today, and an idea born of desperation. Sell the stock, save the farm had become her mantra. A seal of approval from the Acostas would assure the success of the big family event Jess had arranged to showcase her father's prize-winning polo ponies, in the hope of selling at least some of them, in an attempt to stave off the bank and bail her father out of financial trouble.

Jess's father, Jim Slatehome, was a much-loved local

character and everyone from the village had pitched in to help. Using every penny of her savings, as well as a small bequest from her mother, with the invaluable assistance of an army of volunteers, Jess had been able to plan big. Sending out dozens of invitations in the hope of attracting the glitterati of the polo circuit, she had made it her goal to return her father to the spotlight he deserved. Before her mother's death Jim Slatehome had been the go-to trainer and breeder of world-class ponies. Felled by grief, he had retreated from the world and it had taken all Jess's persuasion to persuade him that five years was long enough to shut himself away, and that today marked his return.

Success hovered tantalisingly within their grasp now. Gazing up as the helicopter prepared to land, she knew that if a member of the Acosta family bought some ponies her father would be back on top. But who would step out of that aircraft?

Jess's mouth dried as she thought back ten years to when the gleam of wealth and success blazing from the Acosta brothers had almost blinded her when they arrived on the farm to buy horses. Finding herself alone with Dante Acosta in the stable, some fan girl craziness had prompted her to launch herself at him and plant a kiss on his mouth. He'd stepped away with a huff of disbelief. The scorch of humiliation felt as keen today as it had done then. But she'd never forgotten the kiss. Or that for a moment—and she was never quite sure if she imagined this or not— Dante Acosta had responded.

Jess tensed as the aircraft door swung open. This

was madness, she told herself firmly. And yet she waited, breath held, to see if the fiery superstar of the polo world would descend the steps. She'd followed his career keenly since that first memorable encounter between a naïve seventeen-year-old country girl with a head full of daydreams and a mouth full of cheek and a youth who already boasted the dazzling glamour for which he had since become famous. Dante Acosta's intuition where horses were concerned was said to be second to none, like his success with women. With an army of glamorous female admirers, would he even remember the first time they'd met? Jess's idea of glamour was a night down the pub with her dad, jingling the change in her pocket as she tried to work out if she had enough money to buy him a lemonade.

'Jess—'

She almost jumped out of her skin as she spun around. 'Yes?' It was one of the helpers from the village.

'Your father needs you in the house. I think he's nervous about his welcoming speech.'

'Don't worry. I'll come now and go through it with him.'

It was a relief to drag her attention from the helicopter. Ten years was a long time. These days, she was a fully qualified physiotherapist with a blossoming career, specialising in treating athletes, a fact that would soon bring her face to face with Dante Acosta, whether he appeared today or not. Because of her recent successes in restoring injured athletes to full strength, the Acosta family had chosen Jess to treat their brother's damaged leg, which meant travelling to Spain to Dante's fabulous *estancia*. How he'd feel about the identity of the therapist they'd chosen for him remained to be seen.

She couldn't think about that now. There was today to get though first. Whoever climbed out of the helicopter, it was more likely to be a foreman from one of the Acosta ranches rather than a member of such a wealthy and successful family. Jess's focus was saving the farm, so her father could recover in his own time without upheaval. There were plenty of helpers around to direct the latest arrival to the hospitality marquee where her father was soon to give what Jess passionately hoped would be the sales pitch of his life.

Dante's expression darkened as the cane he was forced to use sank into the claggy mire of a churned-up field. With a vicious curse, he accepted the regrettable conditions. This was no state-of-the-art facility but a beat-up farm in the middle of nowhere.

A farm that boasted some of the best horses in the world, he reminded himself as he ploughed on, which was why he was here. He'd be a fool to miss an opportunity like this. He was always on the lookout for exciting new bloodlines to improve his stock. Aside from playing polo, breeding ponies was his passion, and was the only lure that could drag him out of hibernation after his accident on the polo field. That and the fact that his people had told him the farm was in trouble, and that now would be a good time to buy. He was receiving a constant stream of information from his team to keep him up to speed with any likely competition, as well as likely downsides to a potential purchase. As of now, he was only interested in buying stock.

Another colourful curse heralded a pause as he eased the cramp in his damaged leg. Glancing around, he surveyed the motley throng of farmers, local families and the elite of the horse world, jostling happily alongside each other. They all had one thing in common, which was a deep love of the animals they had come to see, and the sport they provided. A local band added to the upbeat atmosphere. Only Dante's scowl was out of place.

Someone had done a good job of arranging entertainment for the assembled guests, he conceded, taking in the food stalls and all the gaudy trappings of a fairground. This posed a disadvantage for him. He hadn't expected quite so many people. Briefly, he considered the humiliation of the great *El Lobo*, or The Wolf as Dante was known in polo circles, showing himself to the world, staggering along with a cane.

He brushed this off with a snarling curse. Everyone was paparazzo these days. He stood as much chance of being photographed on his *estancia* as he did here.

Dante's stubble-blackened chin lifted at the sound of a young colt neighing. He studied the ponies running free in a field. Young, hard-muscled and spirited, they were perfect. *That* was why he was here.

Really?

Shrugging off the attention of a marshal who had raced to his aid with the offer of a lift in a service vehicle, he asked for Jim Slatehome, the owner of the farm.

'Jim's still in the farmhouse,' the man told him with a shrug. 'Probably running through his speech—'

Dante was already on his way. He hadn't travelled from Spain to indulge in fairground sport or well meaning but ultimately dull parochial chitchat. Nor had he the slightest intention of being last in line when it came to nailing the best stock. A deal would be arranged within the next hour or so, and then he was out of here.

Was he? Was buying new stock the only reason he was here?

The monotony of life since the accident was wearing him down. He needed a distraction. Any distraction. An unsophisticated young country girl stood a chance of taking his mind off the fact that his brothers and sister had gone over his head to arrange a physiotherapist to treat him back in Spain. Dante had discharged himself from hospital prematurely, so his siblings had decided to bring the hospital to him. They knew he wouldn't refuse family. The Acostas were tight and stood by each other always.

Dante's hard mouth tugged with faint amusement as he approached the ramshackle farmhouse with its peeling paint and crooked roof. It was ten years since he'd been here. Was it likely he'd find the little vixen he'd first encountered in the stable? Would she be married now? Engaged? Would he find a significant other by her side? Maybe he should have put his team to work on these details too. The worst he could imagine was that Jim Slatehome's daughter had mellowed to the point of boring, though with her abundance of fiery auburn hair and those flashing emerald eyes he thought it unlikely. One thing was certain. He and Jess Slatehome had unfinished business between them. With this in mind, he planted his cane and lurched on.

'I can't stay long. I have to get back to the marquee to keep people happy until you're ready to give your speech,' Jess explained when her father looked at her with anxiety glistening in his eyes.

He shouldn't be here in the kitchen, nursing a mug of tea, when there were potential buyers for the ponies outside, waiting to meet him. 'Everyone's looking forward to your speech,' she enthused, kneeling by his side at the kitchen table. 'You can do this,' she stated firmly as she got up, wishing she felt as confident as she sounded.

Her father had aged since her mother's death, which was years ago now. It was as if he'd lost hope. He hadn't even shaved today, and his outfit for such a big occasion comprised a random mix of ancient tweed, a greasy flat cap and worn corduroy trousers.

But that was his charm, Jess reminded herself. Jim Slatehome had used to be the go-to trainer and breeder of the best polo ponies in the world, and she was determined to see him back on top again. Her father was every bit as special and unique as the glossiest billionaire newly arrived in his state-of-the-art helicopter, and she loved him to bits.

Yes. Dante was a billionaire. The Acostas were a massively wealthy family, thanks to land holdings, an international tech company, and their skill on a world stage with horses. But this small farm was equally precious to Jess. It had been in her family for generations and she would defend it to the end.

Leaning down to give her father a hug, she was shocked to see tears in his eyes.

'Those ponies mean everything to me, Jess. I can't bear to let them go.'

'But you have to, if you want to keep the farm,' she explained gently. 'Come on; you can do this,' she coaxed.

He gave her a heartbreaking look. 'If you say so. I suppose I'd better go and clean up. I won't let you down, Jess.'

'I know that,' she whispered.

Her father was up and down the stairs in double-quick time and nothing about his appearance had changed, as far as Jess could tell. Apart from his determination, she was relieved to see. 'You're right. I can do this,' he stated firmly. 'I'll go ahead. You stay here. I don't want our guests thinking I need you to prop me up because I've lost confidence in my ponies.'

'Good idea,' Jess agreed.

She was just clearing up their tea things when the kitchen door swung open. She froze on the spot. Breath hitched in her throat. She must have turned ashen, though heat was surging through her veins. Dante Acosta, looking grimmer and tougher than she remembered, was standing in the doorway.

'Dante!'

'Jess…'

Those eyes…that voice…that powerful, compelling presence.

His deep, sonorous voice with its seductive Spanish sibilance rolled across her senses like black velvet brushed lightly, yet so effectively across every sensitive zone she had. His eyes were black pools of experience, while his mouth was a straight, hard line. There was nothing soft or yielding about Dante Acosta—there never had been, she remembered.

Everything in the room disappeared except him. Dante Acosta was the essence of masculinity, the living embodiment of sex. New scars—she guessed they must have been gained on the polo field at the same time as the damage to his leg—cut livid stripes from the upswept tip of one ebony brow to the corner of his firm, cruel mouth. Wind had whipped his thick black hair into such disarray that it had caught on his stubble. A gold hoop glittered in his right ear, adding to a barbaric appearance that seemed at odds with his aura of wealth. But this was no effete billionaire. This was a man of fierce passion and resolve. Beneath his rugged jacket, she knew from the popular press that Dante, like the other members of his polo team, bore a tattoo of a snarling wolf over his heart. This was the insignia of his polo team, Lobos. The team name alone was enough to strike terror in the hearts of their opponents. Lobos was the Spanish word for wolves— a pack of merciless wolves. On the back of Dante's neck, beneath copious glossy whorls of pitch-black hair, he had another tattoo of a skull and crossed mallets, a warning that Team Lobos took no prisoners, and confidently expected to win every match.

A clatter distracted her. The cane he'd discarded by

the door had fallen. Jess frowned. He should be cured by now, with no need for a cane. No wonder his siblings were concerned. Fortunately, they'd sent on his medical records, so she knew the extent of his injury. If Dante hadn't discharged himself from the hospital prematurely, he'd be done with that cane by now.

'Dante,' she said politely, reaching out to shake his hand when he shifted position impatiently. 'How nice to see you again.'

Taking both her hands in a firm grip, he drew her towards him and proceeded to inspect her as if she were a potential purchase like the ponies.

Would you like to examine my teeth? ran through her mind, though she knew that for the sake of any potential purchase she had to mind her manners and remain calm. That wasn't easy when she was practically drowning in charisma, so she closed her eyes.

'Let me look at you…'

That voice again. She jerked her hands free. Dante Acosta was a exciting force of nature but he knew it and had no shame when it came to wielding his power. It was up to Jess to resist him. *If she could.* She hadn't made too good a job of resisting him ten years ago and, seeing him again, she was inclined to forgive her teenage self.

Her hands had felt so small and safe in his—which was all part of the illusion. This was no time to be seduced by a man with more money than Croesus and the morals of an alley cat. How would that help her father? If there was one thing she'd learned since returning home to take care of her father, it was that vultures were always circling. Everyone was out for a deal. Why should Dante Acosta be any different?

'Jess?'

'Apologies. Sorry. I'm forgetting my manners. Welcome—welcome to Bell Farm. Would you like a drink? I expect you've had a long journey.'

'From Spain?' A casual shrug of his massive shoulders hinted at executive travel in the most luxurious of circumstances. 'Not so bad.'

Why did everything about Dante Acosta make her feel like this? She was always blasé about men. Because none could compare with Dante Acosta, as she had discovered ten years ago when she kissed him.

'Tea, surely?' she said to distract herself from the insistent throb between her legs.

'Can't stand the stuff.'

'Oh.' That took her by surprise. 'Something else, perhaps?'

'What have you got?'

From any other lips those words could be taken as an innocent request for a verbal menu. When they came from Dante Acosta the prompt was laden with deadly charm. 'Whatever you like,' she said brightly. 'The stalls outside sell pretty much everything.'

As one corner of his mouth tugged slightly as if to say *Touché*, she knew he'd feel like velvet steel beneath her hands.

Had nothing changed in ten years? Was she still as reckless?

Far from it, Jess told herself firmly. She was no longer a reckless teen but a medical professional who had left a successful career at a leading London teaching hospital to come home to help her father.

'I'm sure you want to see my father, not me,' she said pleasantly. 'Would you like me to take you to him?'

'There's no need,' Dante said with a narrow-eyed look. 'I'll find my own way.'

As he turned, Jess felt as if she'd been appraised and discarded. That was fine. This wasn't about her. She'd arranged the event with the specific intention of attracting an Acosta or the like, someone with a deep love of horses and plenty of money to bail her father out of trouble by buying up his stock. If Dante didn't bite she'd have to find someone who would.

So, Dante mused as he wove his way through the crowd to reach the show ring—if a hastily tidied up paddock with a rickety fence could be described as such a thing— the little vixen he remembered had matured into a beautiful, understated, though rather too serious woman. He missed the mischief in Jess's eyes, as well as the excessively impulsive nature that had prompted her, at the tender age of seventeen, to stand on tiptoe to plant a kiss on his lips.

His senses surged, remembering. He had reined in those senses then and would do so again. He wasn't here to waste time on a serious-minded woman. He wasn't ready to take any woman seriously. Why restrict his diet when the menu was so varied?

Leaning on the hated cane, he paused to greet some fellow polo players. Jess had attracted a motley crowd, from locals to minor royals and celebrities as well as sightseers from far and wide. Towering men in black suits with earpieces and suspicious bulges beneath their jackets followed hot on the heels of a well-known sheikh. Dante had never relied on security personnel for his safety, preferring to rely on his own skills to protect him.

One career had foundered while the other had soared, he mused, moving on when he spotted Jess walking arm in arm with her father. His team had informed him that the farm was in serious financial trouble. They were already working on the ins and outs and would advise him on the questions he'd pose before the day was out.

One thing was certain. Jess had left her job and risked her career to come here to save her father and the farm. She was unusually determined, and he admired that.

He also detested loose ends. If Jess hadn't been seventeen ten years ago, who knew what might have happened between them?

The marquee was already crowded by the time he entered. He recognised more horse breeders, trainers and players like himself jostling to get to the front under Jim Slatehome's nose. He wouldn't have it all his own way today. There would be stiff competition for the better horses.

So he'd go one better.

He could offer double—triple—what anyone else could without feeling a pinch. He could easily afford it. Jim had sold him some good stock in the past, and what he'd seen of the ponies in the field so far suggested Jim had never really gone away, but had made himself invisible so he could nurse his grief.

The urge to help Jim Slatehome overwhelmed him suddenly. To fend off the competition meant putting something else in the pot. After the most recent text from his team an idea was already brewing. How would Jess take his idea, if he went ahead and bought the farm? Not well, he suspected as watched her standing like a protection officer at her father's side. It had cost her everything to be here, financially, career-wise, every which way. His team had filled him in on the details. She'd qualified top of her class as a physiotherapist specialising in sports injuries. Her first job was at a prestigious teaching hospital in London, but she'd given that up to go freelance, which could be tricky. Rumour said she was successful. If she was as good as her reputation suggested, she could guarantee an endless stream of patients from the battleground of polo alone. The thought of those soft hands tracking right up his legs was—

Out of bounds, Dante told himself sternly. He was here for business and nothing else. He'd seen the vixen and satisfied his curiosity, and that had to be enough.

Thankfully, the Sheikh sidled up to him at that moment and as they got talking about horses Dante grew more determined than ever to win the day. He'd handle Jess's objections. As her father mounted the podium and began his speech, Dante stared at Jess.

CHAPTER TWO

HER FATHER'S SPEECH went well. He seemed buoyed up. Maybe the brief chats he'd managed to snatch with Dante had served as a reminder that Jim Slatehome had once been great and would be so again. That was Jess's dearest hope as she congratulated her father, and prompted him to start discussing specific ponies with potential buyers.

'Be patient,' he implored. 'I'm going to speak to Dante while you circulate amongst our guests. Keep them happy while I'm away. This talk is important, Jess,' he added with a significant look.

'I'd rather stay with you.' She glanced at Dante, standing waiting for her father to join him, and felt the same punch to her senses, added to which was the fear that they were cooking something up between them. Dante's expression betrayed nothing beyond a cool stare in her direction.

'This is still my farm, Jess.'

The reminder struck home. Anything she could do to see her father back on top had to be all right with Jess. 'Promise me you won't do anything silly before you and I have talked it through.'

'Like fortune-telling in a tent under the name of Skylar?' her father suggested, lifting one bushy brow.

'You've got me there,' Jess admitted wryly as she checked her watch to make sure she had time to chat to the guests before she was due to inhabit the small gaudy tent that would house the mysterious Skylar.

'Go,' her father prompted urgently.

With a last suspicious glance at the tall, dark man in the shadows who made her heart pound like crazy, she planted a kiss on her father's cheek and did as he said.

The day had turned cold Jess discovered when she stepped out of the marquee. Or maybe apprehension was chilling her. The sky was blue. There wasn't a cloud to be seen and if the air wasn't exactly tropical it was still warm for the time of year in this part of England. In honour of the heatwave Jess had dressed in a thick sweater, a down gilet and a padded coat. Even in summer it could be frigid on the moors.

It would have been a great time to appreciate how well the event was going, had it not been for the turmoil in her head. Seeing Dante again had affected her more than she could ever have imagined, bringing back those few moments in the stable ten years ago, when just for a moment Dante had responded, spoiling her for all other men. There had been men—of course there had, she was almost twenty-seven—serious men, driven by the need to educate; nerdy men obsessed with their phones; *bon viveurs* whose sole aim in life appeared to be preserving their bodies by pickling them in alcohol; gym bunnies and those she would have been wiser to swerve. But none compared to the brigand with atti-tude, known to one and all as The Wolf.

And now he was even more attractive. And more elusive. With homes across the world, Dante Acosta could pitch up anywhere.

Face it, the gulf between them was a mile wide.

Jess threw herself back into chatting with as many of their visitors as she could. Her reaction to seeing Dante again was an overreaction.

Tell that to her heart. Tell that to her body. Tell her stubborn mind, that doggedly refused to accept it. Making her excuses to the smiling guests, she moved on. What better way to take her mind off Dante Acosta than to get stuck into some fortune-telling, Jess con-cluded wryly as she headed back to the house to change into Skylar's costume.

Perhaps she could tell her own fortune. Although surely that could easily be predicted. Dante Acosta could, and probably would, disappear from her life again as swiftly as he had recently appeared.

The ground was hard with frost and the views be-tween the field and the farmhouse far-reaching and mesmerising. Jess stopped briefly to admire them, and to chat silently to her mother, as she so often did. Her mother had been dead for more than five years but her presence remained constant in Jess's heart.

She reviewed the promises she'd made—to complete her studies, to look after her father and make sure he kept the farm. Generations of farming ran through her father's blood. He'd have no purpose in life and nowhere to live, her mother had impressed upon her, so these were sacred vows as far as Jess was concerned.

She had never cried at the loss of her mother, Jess realised as the wind whipped her face, prompting her to move on. Her father had cried enough for both of them, but Jess had bottled up her grief deep inside because her father's tears had solved nothing. They hadn't brought her mother back or sent the bank packing. She had to save him, as she'd promised, and so she mourned silently and dealt firmly with the bank. So far she'd managed to stave off repossession of the farm, but for how long? A good sale today might postpone the inevitable, but it wouldn't solve the problem, which meant there was a possibility they might have to sell off some of the land.

Jess's mood lifted when she turned to see how many people were grouped around her father. He looked as happy as she'd ever seen him, dispensing advice and answering questions. Jim Slatehome was back! People in the horse world who mattered were hanging on his every word.

But there was no sign of Dante. Had he lost interest? There was no time to dwell. She had to prepare to tell fortunes.

When Jess came downstairs after changing into Skylar's colourful costume of voluminous, ankle-length skirt strewn with bells and a heavy fringed shawl to wrap around her shoulders, Dante and her father were sitting in the kitchen. The way the two men fell silent the moment she walked in made her instantly suspicious. What were they up to?

Dante's incredulous stare made her self-conscious. She doubted he'd seen many women with scarves and bells tied around their hair, dressed in shapeless clothes that looked as if they belonged in a jumble sale—which was actually where she'd found them. Even in jeans and workmanlike boots, he managed to look like a king amongst men. But her father seemed happy enough and what else mattered?

'I'm doubly glad I came,' Dante murmured, tongue firmly planted in his cheek.

'And we're extremely glad you could find time to come to our event, aren't we, Dad?' she responded politely through gritted teeth.

Her father was definitely hiding something. She knew that guilty look. And she had only succeeded in sounding ridiculous, like Eliza Doolittle trying to please Professor Higgins, when Dante deserved no such consideration with that smirk on his face. 'It's nice to see you again,' she added, aiming for casual.

'*Nice?*' Dante queried in a deep, husky tone that ran tremors through every part of her. Why wasn't her father helping out? Why must she deal with this man on her own?

'Is the apron to protect you from the kittens?' Dante asked straight-faced.

His comment launched her back to the past and the first time they'd met, when Jess had been caring for a litter of kittens. One of them had chosen the precise moment Dante walked into the stables to pee down her front.

'It's part of my costume,' she said primly.

When she'd almost lost hope that her father might

find some way to ease the tension between Jess and Dante he sprang back to life. 'Come on,' he urged, standing up. 'I'll escort you to the fortune-telling tent. I might even be one of your first clients.'

'Do you read tea leaves?' Dante enquired, still holding back on that laugh.

'Jess is a dab hand with a crystal ball,' her father explained, oblivious to the war of hard stares currently being exchanged between Jess and Dante. 'She's great at telling fortunes. You should try her.'

'I might do that,' Dante murmured with a long look at Jess.

He infuriated her but melted her from the inside out too, which was inconvenient. Dante Acosta was a storming force of nature that commanded her attention whether she wanted him to or not.

Jess stalked ahead of her father to the fortune-telling tent. She was annoyed with her wilful body for responding so enthusiastically to Dante. Her nipples had tightened into taut, cheeky buds, while her lips felt swollen and her breasts felt heavy. And that was the least of it.

The sky was clouding over but in spite of the rapidly worsening weather there was a long line waiting for Jess outside Skylar's tent. There was nothing like a bit of supernatural hocus pocus to put the seal of success on a day out like this. Jess's father really believed she'd got a gift, while her mother had dubbed her Skylar years ago, saying Jess should have a magic name to go with her gift. Jess had always suspected that this was just her mother's way of putting steel in the spine of a painfully shy child.

It must have worked, she concluded, thinking back ten years to when she'd launched herself at the most eligible bachelor on the planet.

Ten years on, was she running away from him?

She glanced over her shoulder before ducking inside the tent. No one was following. Dante was as disinterested in her now as he had been then. It was time to forget him and get on with the job.

For the first time ever he was having trouble concentrating as he struck a deal with Jess's father. Jess remained on his mind as he wove his way through the crowd to discover what his future held.

Okay, he was a cynic when it came to telling fortunes, but that didn't stop him wanting to see Jess. Ten years back, he'd been twenty-two and dismissive of potential mates unless they satisfied his demanding criteria. Jess with her paint-free face, scraped-back hair and clothes smelling of cat pee, not to mention the mouth on her like a paint-stripper, had been as far from his ideal as it was possible to get.

Until she kissed him.

That had been one big surprise, and a kick to his senses, reminding him not to overlook something when it was right under his nose.

The long line in front of Skylar's tent stopped him in his tracks. He wasn't a man to queue.

With that kiss he'd had the good sense to curtail ten years ago nagging at his mind, he wasn't a man to wait either. No longer a naïve teen, Jess was a beautiful and intriguing woman. Shapely and soft on the outside, the intrigue came from the will of steel that blazed from her eyes.

That same determination had enabled her to save the farm. According to his team, Jess had no funds other than her meagre savings. She'd stripped these bare to put on this show and save her father. Using persuasion, and bartering her physiotherapy services where necessary, she had managed to recruit practically every member of the village to ensure today's success. The result was this confidence-boosting exercise for Jim Slatehome that should put him firmly back on the map.

He stopped in front of the small, gaudily decorated tent. A large banner hung from the turret, declaring boldly: *Skylar Slates—fortune-teller to the stars!* His cynical smile was back. He guessed he qualified. Now his only problem was how to crash the line.

Retracing his steps, he bought a pack of water from a stall. 'I can handle it,' he snapped at the woman behind the counter when she gazed at his stick. Clamping the unwieldy bundle beneath one arm, he stabbed his stick into the ground and set his sights on his goal.

'Water for the fortune-teller,' he announced as he approached the ever-lengthening line in front of Skylar's tent. 'To keep her voice running smoothly,' he explained, mustering every bit of his rusty charm. The throng parted like the Red Sea to allow the unfortunate man with his lurching gait to move through them with his awkward burden. He vowed on the spot that this would be the one and only time that he viewed his injury as a benefit.

Having arrived at his destination, he rested his cane against the canvas wall and, drawing the flap aside, he ducked his head and walked in.

'Excuse me,' Jess rapped with the paint-stripping look he remembered so well. 'I'll call you in when I'm free.'

'Oh, no, no, please,' the woman seated at the table opposite Jess insisted, getting up to make way for him.

'What do you think you're doing?' Jess demanded, shooting emerald fire his way.

He would have known those flashing eyes anywhere, and those lips that formed a perfect Cupid's bow of possibility. The urge to taste the creamy perfection of Jess's rain-washed skin and rasp his stubble against its soft perfection was overwhelming right now. But he had business to transact. 'I'm here to cross your palm with silver and your lips with a bottle of water,' he explained.

'You're asking me to tell your fortune?' she asked with surprise.

Having put the bottles down, he delved in his pocket for some coins to toss on the table, but his casual air was halted by a bolt of pain.

'You'd better sit down,' she said. 'Where's your cane?'

'Thank you for reminding me.'

The look she gave him told him she understood what it must have cost him to come here today with his cane, in front of all these people. And yet what was pride when there was a deal to be done? They measured each other for a few moments and then she reached out to take his hand. Full marks to Jess, he conceded, for retaining her composure, and remembering that he might save the farm. She had guts, and to spare, he reflected.

'Are you sure you want this?' she asked.

'I wouldn't be here if I didn't,' he assured her, while his senses prompted him to take her somewhere where they could be alone. 'Why does that surprise you?'

'I can't believe Señor Acosta is incapable of predicting his own future.'

'Oh, but I can.' He held Jess's gaze locked in his and was rewarded when she blushed deeply.

'You crashed the line,' she scolded.

'I did,' he agreed with a shrug. How beautiful she was, even with what looked like a piece of Christmas tinsel wrapped around her head. Her hair glowed like fire in the soft light of a lamp, over which she'd draped a piece of red chiffon, while her eyes were deep pools of unfathomable green.

'Stop staring at me. I'm supposed to be reading you, not the other way around.'

'Then get on with it,' he suggested.

She reached across and rattled an old biscuit tin that had an opening cut in the top. 'Put your money in here—those pieces of silver,' she reminded him.

'Of course...'

He added a few more coins to those he'd already tossed down on the table. She still held out the tin. 'A twenty should do it,' she prompted bluntly.

'Twenty?' He pulled his head back with surprise.

'Can't you afford it?'

Her lips curved in the first real smile he'd seen and her eyes danced with laughter. That was the Jess he remembered from the stable ten years ago—feisty and free to speak her mind, rather than constrained by the fact that he might be her father's last hope when it came to saving the farm. He preferred this Jess.

'Every penny goes directly to charity,' she explained. 'Nothing I take in this tent will be kept for the farm.'

'Then you can have all my cash.' Levering himself to his feet, he reached into his back pocket to bring out a wad of notes. He fed them into her tin. 'This had better be worth it,' he warned.

But fortune-telling wasn't on Jess's mind now. 'Your leg,' she said with concern. 'You really must agree to treatment. Please don't be stubborn if the appropriate therapy is offered to you, or you could be left with a permanent limp.'

'Did you see that in your crystal ball?' he demanded edgily as he sat down again.

'I don't need a crystal ball to see that. I'm a fully qualified physiotherapist, more than used to dealing with injuries like yours. Which is why I can tell you with authority that you can't afford to leave this any longer,' she added before he could get a word in.

'Well, thank you for your advice, *Skylar*,' he gritted out, 'but that's not what I'm paying you for. What *can* you see in that crystal ball…if anything?'

'A very difficult man,' she fired back.

They glared at each other, and for a good few moments fire flashed between them. Just like ten years ago, it seemed they were destined to strike sparks off each other whenever they met.

'You'll have to be quiet or I can't concentrate,' she said.

'That's the best line I've heard yet,' he muttered as he settled back in his seat.

But Jess did appear to compose herself, before dipping her head and cupping her hands around the ball. His groin tightened at the sight of slender fingers caressing the inanimate object. This was ridiculous. He'd never reacted like this.

Then Jess looked up and made things ten times worse. Her green eyes flayed him before she even spoke, and then she exploded, 'No way!' Pushing the crystal ball away, she snapped, 'This session is at an end.'

'I'm sorry?' he queried dryly. 'Did I miss something, only you don't seem to have told me anything yet.'

Standing up, she stared pointedly at the exit. 'There are people waiting outside. Thank you for your contribution, but—'

'But get lost?' he suggested. 'Is that any way to treat a prospective buyer?'

'If you'd seen what I've seen, you'd be begging to go.'

'All that money and I don't get a second chance?'

'Believe me. You don't want a second chance,' Jess assured him.

He felt a frisson of something as he stared at her, but dismissed it out of hand. No one could foretell the future. This was all an act.

'I can tell you one thing,' she said. 'Like your namesake The Wolf, you should shed your old winter coat, to be ready for spring and changes.'

'Claptrap.'

'Is it?' she challenged, eyes flashing fire as they refocused on his face. 'Or are you afraid to face what lies ahead?'

'Frightened?' he queried with a short, humourless laugh. 'Are we talking about therapy for my leg?'

'Might be. You must accept treatment before it's too late.'

'Is that what you do?' He gestured around the tent. 'Offer advice under the guise of fortune-telling?'

Jess sighed softly. 'Is that so terrible? Sometimes it's the only way people will hear and take in what they need to. I don't mean any harm.'

'I'm sure you don't,' he agreed grimly. 'But, thank you very much, my siblings have arranged something for me, so you don't need to worry about my leg.'

'That's good news,' she said.

He grunted. 'Don't keep your other mugs waiting.'

'Let's hope they're politer than you.'

But Jess said this with a smile and a genuinely concerned look, which made it hard to remain angry for long. The most annoying teen had grown into a most annoying, hot as hell woman.

CHAPTER THREE

So Jess was unmarried and unattached. Why that should please him, he couldn't say. After all, it wasn't as though he was interested in a relationship with her. Still, his conversation with her father when he returned to the farmhouse hadn't been solely confined to business, and Jim Slatehome had confided that Jess was single. Jim was proud of his daughter, and eager to talk about what she'd achieved. 'Without anyone's help,' he told Dante. 'I just feel sometimes that I'm holding her back. Jess has a big heart. She should share it with a family of her own.'

He fell silent, and the pause was only broken by the crackle of the fire and an old clock ticking on the mantelpiece. And then Jess walked in.

Her father visibly brightened. 'Come and join us,' he said, pulling out a chair.

'When I've showered and changed,' she promised.

Without sparing him a glance, she gathered up the mud-soaked hem of her skirt and dashed upstairs.

She didn't take long to return. Still glowing from the shower, she radiated energy and purpose, and even in a pair of old jeans, scrappy slippers and a nondescript top she was beautiful. She'd made no attempt to impress, which was probably what impressed him most of all.

'Talks between you two go well?' she prompted with seeming unconcern, but there was an edge of tension in her voice.

'Extremely well,' her father enthused, which only succeeded in making Jess pale.

'Well?' she pressed. 'Aren't you going to tell me what you've decided? Are you buying the horses, Dante?'

'All in good time,' her father promised, thwarting Jess's attempt to turn the spotlight on him. 'Deal or no deal, Dante's still our guest, and he doesn't want to go over the details time and time again. We'll have plenty of chance to discuss it when he's gone.'

Jess's jaw worked as if she disagreed, but she sensibly remained silent. The chance of a deal could not be risked, and she was wise enough to know this.

'Did Skylar do well in the end?' he asked to break the ice when she sat with them in silence.

'You tell me,' she said, fixing him with a look. 'Did you find me convincing?'

'I mean financially,' he explained, matching her no-nonsense look and raising it with serious concern of his own. 'You said it was for charity, so I hope you raked in lots of money.'

'Your generous donation helped,' she admitted. 'I don't think we've ever raised so much.'

'You'll have to come back every year,' her father put in.

Jess drew in a settling breath. 'Yes, why don't you?'

'I intend to.'

'That's good,' her father exclaimed, thumping the table in his enthusiasm. 'Now we'll never lose contact again. The day's been a huge success, and that's all down to you, Jess.'

'And your wonderful ponies, and our helpers from the village,' she insisted, shaking off her father's praise as if she didn't deserve it.

'Sometimes, just say thank you,' he advised good-humouredly.

She shot him a narrow-eyed look, and now her father looked guilty as hell.

'What's going on?' Jess challenged.

'Going on?' her father echoed in a splutter. 'Absolutely nothing,' he protested. 'We've struck a wonderful deal.'

As if to confirm this, the sound of helicopters roaring overhead prevented conversation for a while.

'So all the other potential purchasers are leaving,' Jess commented, staring skywards. She stabbed a look into his eyes. 'So, it's all down to you.'

'Stop fretting, Jess,' her father insisted. 'Dante bought all the horses.'

'All of them?' she murmured, frowning. 'Why do I get the feeling there's something more?'

'Shake his hand, Jess. The farm is saved. The deal is done.'

If looks could kill, the Acostas would be short one member of the family. Jess could afford to show her true feelings now. Standing up, she extended her hand for him to shake. As he captured the tiny fist in his

giant paw he was surprised to discover how strong
she was. This was no soft, vulnerable individual, but
a worthy opponent. That pleased him. He was tired of
sycophants and creeps. Extreme wealth came with dis-
advantages, not least of which was its effect on other
people. He couldn't count the times he'd been fawned
over, when all he required was to be tested and judged
on his merits as a man.

'You can let me go now,' she said.

Realising they were still hand-clasping, he released
her. 'Skylar was right about one thing,' he admitted.

'Oh?' Jess's green stare pierced his.

'The deal I struck with your father marks the start
of a new chapter in my life.'

'Does that happen every time you buy a few horses?'
she demanded suspiciously.

'These aren't just any horses,' her father interrupted,
clearly keen to bring Jess's line of questioning to an
end. 'These are Slatehome ponies.'

Jess hummed, her suspicion by no means satisfied.

'How did you come by the name Skylar?' he enquired, to break the tension between them when, at
her father's insistence, Jess sat down again.

'It was a nickname my mother dreamed up for me
when I was heading into my shell and she wanted me
to shine. She said Skylar was a witchy name for people
with The Sight and it would give me special powers.
We laughed about it, and I never felt shy again, because I had this other person inside me: Skylar Slates,
fortune-teller extraordinaire. Even now the name re-
minds me of my mother and the many ways she had to

make people feel good about themselves. That was her gift. Skylar's predictions try to encourage hopes and dreams and soothe worries. It seems to help,' she added with a self-deprecating shrug, 'but that's all thanks to my mother.'

'You must miss her terribly.'

'I do.'

For a second he saw that, in one area at least, Jess was vulnerable. The raw wound of loss had never healed. It had been some time since her mother's death. He didn't know exactly. He was guilty of losing touch with anything outside his privileged cocoon and had become even more isolated since the accident.

'My ancestors on my mother's side were *gitanos*,' he revealed. 'Mountain people. Some would call them gypsies. Many of them have The Sight.'

'Jess is shrewd and intuitive, but her magic is confined to making the best cup of tea in Yorkshire,' her father interrupted with his broadest hint yet.

'Make mine coffee,' he reminded Jess.

Having arranged three mugs on the range, she absent-mindedly filled them all with tea from the pot. 'Oh, look at me!' she exclaimed with impatience.

He was having difficulty doing anything else.

After making a coffee for Dante she left the two men in the kitchen. She didn't mean to listen in on her return. Who ever did? Her father was telling Dante it was time for him to say goodbye to the last of his guests, and the moment the kitchen door closed behind him Dante was on the phone. 'It's all done,' he said.

'Everything wrapped up to my satisfaction. Notify the lawyers and have the contract drawn up ASAP.'

The covering certificate for each individual pony was already to hand, Jess reasoned with a frown, together with all the requirements for any valuable pedigree horse changing hands. This included a DNA hair sample from both the Sire and Dam to confirm the pony's parentage. The deed of sale was a straightforward matter that would be handled by her father's lawyer. So why was more paperwork necessary?

She barely had chance to reason this through when there was a crash in the kitchen, followed by an earth-shattering curse. Bursting in, she rushed to Dante's side. 'Let me help you up.' Crossing the kitchen without his cane, he'd tripped over a chair leg.

When he snapped tersely, 'My cane, please,' she let it go. The loss of face on a daily basis for a man like Dante Acosta had to be monumental. If he refused treatment, nothing would change.

Handing him the cane, she stood back.

'And no bloody lectures about accepting treatment,' he warned.

'Just do it,' she suggested mildly.

This was rewarded by a grunt. 'Let me look at that leg,' she insisted. 'You might have caused more damage when you fell. Please,' she added when Dante looked at her in silence.

'Very well,' he agreed reluctantly.

She knelt on the floor in front of him, while Dante sat down on the chair. Rolling up the leg of his jeans, she quickly reassured herself that no further damage had been done.

'*Gracias*,' he grated out when she told him this, and got up.

'It's my job,' she said with a shrug. 'Here,' she said when he began to rise. 'Don't forget your cane.'

He took hold of it, and for some reason she didn't let go. For a few potent seconds they were connected by a length of polished wood. Then, to her horror, he began to reel her in. She could let go but she didn't, and Dante only stopped when their faces were almost touching. Closing her eyes, she wondered if she'd have the strength to resist him, or if she would follow the urges of a body that had been denied release and satisfaction for far too long.

'You like playing with fire, don't you, Skylar?' Dante murmured,

She dropped the cane like a red-hot poker. 'I'm trying to help.'

'Yourself?' Dante suggested.

'I don't know what you mean.'

'I think you do,' he argued. 'And if you play with my fire you will definitely get burned. Is that what you want?'

She gave a short huff of incredulity. 'My interest in you is purely professional.'

Furious with herself for succumbing to the notorious Acosta charm, she crossed the room and reached for her coat. Ramming her feet into boots, she went to join her father in saying goodbye to their guests, leaving the mighty Dante Acosta to sort himself out.

* * *

He refused to go unless Jess came with him. She plagued his mind and tormented his body, and until she agreed to accompany him to Spain he wasn't going anywhere.

How was that supposed to happen when they weren't on speaking terms?

He'd find a way.

Confined to the house long enough, he gritted out a curse and heaved himself to his feet.

He found Jess riding in the outside arena. From the look of concentration on her face he guessed she found solace as he did, by twinning her soul with a horse. Animal and human moving as one, with scarcely a visible adjustment on Jess's part to suggest she was directing the intricate moves, was the most healing activity he could think of. She was a master equestrian. He should have expected that. He was impressed.

Worthy sentiments were soon surpassed by a flash of triumph as he reflected that all this belonged to him now. Jess didn't know the extent of his deal with her father. Jim Slatehome had asked that they keep it between themselves for the time being that Dante had bought the farm and everything on it. 'She can be difficult, our Jess,' her father had explained. 'She's had a tough time. I'll know when it's the right time to tell her. Until then, say nothing. I don't want her upset after all she's done.'

Triumph yielded to lust as Jess brought her pony alongside him at the fence. 'This is our best horse. Her name is Moon,' she informed him.

'You handle her well.'

She smiled. 'High praise indeed.'

'I mean it.'

This was possibly the first relaxed conversation they'd had, and it allowed him to press forward with his plan; rather than alienating Jess, he had to form a connection with a woman who could be useful to him. There were always vacancies for top-class riders in one of his teams. 'Show me what she can do,' he encouraged.

'I just did.'

'Please,' he coaxed, dialling up the charm.

'As it's you…' But she was smiling.

He leaned on a fencepost as Jess put the promising mare through her paces. The pony could be difficult and liked to show off. Sensing he was watching her, Moon kicked out her back legs and bucked. Jess remained perfectly balanced throughout.

'Good job,' he said when she returned to his side.

'I love the challenge of a spirited pony,' she enthused as she reined in.

'I love a challenge full stop.'

She blushed.

'You've got a good seat.' She had a great seat. It would fit his hands perfectly. 'Do you play?'

'I take it you're referring to polo?'

'What else?' he asked, throwing her a surprised look.

'I used to play,' she admitted, 'but I'm usually too tired by the end of each day, so I read instead, play the piano, or crash out in front of a soap.'

'Everyone needs fresh air. You should get out more.'

'Says you?' she jibed.

Humour drained from his eyes. It was common knowledge that Dante Acosta had been housebound since discharging himself from hospital, and that this was his first appearance in public. 'Don't make me regret accepting the invitation to come here today.'

Jess had the good sense to say nothing. She didn't need to. Her eyes spoke eloquently, telling him, *I'm not sure yet what's in it for you, but you would have left by now if the answer was nothing.*

'What are you doing?' she asked as he opened the gate to join her in the paddock.

'I want to see Moon close up for myself.'

'Take care; she bites.'

'You or the horse?'

'She won't like your cane.'

'Then may I suggest you dismount and hand her over to a groom?'

'A groom?' Jess intoned. 'Where do you think you are? This is a working farm, not some billionaire's playground.'

His hackles lifted. 'I live on a working ranch. My business life and home life are very different. Do you want me to trial her or not?'

'You already own her.'

'I do.'

'Then she's all yours,' Jess said with a shrug, but as she turned he saw that accepting the inevitable wasn't easy for Jess. She loved these animals and couldn't bear the thought of never seeing them again.

'Be careful,' she said as he vaulted into the saddle using only the strength of his arms. 'Moon can be tricky.'

'You care?' he asked as he soothed the horse.

'I care about Moon,' she told him.

'Hey, *querida*, let's see what you can do,' he whispered, adding soothing words in Spanish. The pony's flattened ears pricked up at the sound of his warm, encouraging tone and she didn't disappoint, though each swerve and bounce jangled his damaged nerve-endings.

'A good enough reason to accept treatment?' Jess suggested as he made sure not to stumble as he dismounted, by taking the weight on his one good leg.

'She'll make the first team,' he said, ignoring her question.

'Your reputation is well deserved,' she commented as he handed over the reins.

'Do you mean I can ride?' he suggested with a grin.

'Like a master,' she said frankly.

'Your father has lost nothing when it comes to his gift for breeding and training some of the best horses in the world, and some of it's rubbed off on you.'

'Only some of it?' she said, smiling.

'All right…' With a conciliatory gesture, he smiled too. That connection he'd wanted was on the rise.

'Do you want to trial any more ponies?' Jess asked.

'I'll leave that to my grooms. I trust a practised eye and intuition.' And his leg couldn't take any more today.

'How will you transport the ponies to Spain?' Jess

asked with concern, glancing at his helicopter in the next field.

'The same way my grooms arrived today. In a specially adapted jet,' he revealed.

'You haven't wasted much time,' she observed suspiciously.

'I never do.' He let the silence hang for a few seconds before adding, 'You should come with me when I go back to Spain—to settle the horses,' he went on before she could argue.

'Can't your grooms do that?'

'I thought you'd like to do it. The ponies know you. They don't know my grooms yet.'

She couldn't argue with that, but she did raise one objection. 'I have work commitments.'

So it wasn't a flat no, he registered with satisfaction.

'And luckily they dovetail nicely.'

Well, that was a surprise. 'So you're saying yes?'

'I believe I am,' Jess confirmed, as if all the advantage in coming to Spain with him was on her side.

CHAPTER FOUR

JESS HAD NEVER seen her father looking so relaxed. He looked ten years younger, as if all his worries were behind him. She'd just sat down when Dante entered the kitchen.

'It was good of you to judge the children's pony race,' her father exclaimed as Dante sat next to her.

Tingling apart, she was surprised to learn that the great Dante Acosta had joined in to such an extent. 'I didn't know you'd been so busy,' she admitted.

'I enjoyed it,' Dante confessed with a sideways look that heated her up from the inside out. 'We'll have to make it an annual event. You were busy being Skylar,' he reminded her.

'It must have been a bit different to your usual afternoon,' her father ventured with a laugh.

'I enjoyed every moment,' Dante assured him with a look at Jess.

'Dante picked prize winners in each different age group,' her father revealed, 'and spent extra time with a little girl who forfeited her race to go back and help her younger brother.'

Saint Dante? Jess reflected, amused in a good way.

What Dante had done today had put him in the spot-light, which couldn't have been easy for him, but the children would have loved having one of polo's biggest stars taking an interest in them.

'That was very good of you,' she said frankly.

'So. Transport tomorrow,' he said.

'*Tomorrow?*' Jess hadn't expected to be leaving the farm quite so soon.

'I don't waste time. Remember?' Dante prompted.

Only an Acosta could make things work as fast as this. Jess's spine prickled. What was she getting into?

'You'll find my jet comfortable, and the ponies will have the best care possible.' Dante was continuing as if there was nothing unusual in making a decision one minute, a plan the next, and executing that plan the following day. 'A vet and her assistant will be on duty throughout, while my grooms will be in constant atten-dance. You'll have very little to do, other than to keep a watchful eye on the animals and inform my grooms if they have any quirks or preferences.'

'But I must be home for Christmas.' Dry-mouthed and backtracking fast as the extent of her commitment to a man she hardly knew, who lived in a country she wasn't used to, hit home, Jess added, 'I won't leave my father on his own.'

'How old do you think I am, Jess?' her father pro-tested. 'You have to stay in Spain until you're sure those animals are happily settled. You know how much they mean to me.'

And there was that contract she'd signed for the

Acostas, which could keep her in Spain a lot longer than that. 'I'll be back for Christmas,' she stated firmly.

Jess managed to convince herself that this trip made good sense. She was going to reassure herself and her father that the horses were properly settled. That was important. She also had to find the right opportunity to break the news to Dante that she was his new therapist. He wouldn't thank her. The regime she'd mapped out would be punishing. He'd left it so long—too long—that only the most intense therapy would stand a chance of effecting change. Even then, there was no guarantee of a full recovery.

With that situation unresolved, she turned her thoughts to something she could influence, which was care of the horses. 'I have no idea how the ponies will react until we're in the air,' she admitted honestly. 'I'll feel more confident when we land, especially if your facilities are as good as I hear they are—'

'They are,' Dante assured her.

'Then I don't foresee any problems.'

'And I'm happy to welcome you on board.'

He was proud of his jet. He owned a couple of smaller aircraft as well as several helicopters, one of which was kept on his yacht, but this huge aircraft with its custom fittings and long-range capabilities was his particular pride and joy. It enabled him to be anywhere in the world on a whim—with or without his horses. There were stalls rivalling any in the world on the lower level, and a fully staffed veterinary surgery in case of emergency. The upper level was more like a super-luxe apartment than anything resembling a plane. One of the foremost interior designers had kitted it out to Dante's specific instructions to include bedrooms, a galley manned by a Michelin starred chef, as well as a couple of luxurious bathrooms. In addition to this, he had a full working office and a spacious lounge where he could relax.

'Wow,' Jess gasped when they had boarded and she could look around. 'This isn't so much an aircraft as a flying palace. And you need all this…why?'

'Because I'm a very busy man.'

'I can see that,' she agreed, viewing the tech in his office as he took her on the tour.

'Would you have my horses walk home?'

'Of course not, but it does seem…how can I put this?…very big for one man.'

'How kind of you to highlight my regrettable bachelor status,' he mocked lightly.

'Don't mention it,' Jess returned, matching his tone and adding a grin.

At least she was relaxed. 'Make yourself at home,' he invited. Cabin attendants were standing by with trays of the finest Cristal champagne, as well as delicious canapés designed to tempt a flagging appetite.

'I'd rather see the horses settled, if you don't mind,' Jess told him matter-of-factly, managing a warm smile for the attendants at the same time. 'Could you show me the way, please?' she added.

'Of course.' There were many things he'd like to show Jess, and not with stabling as his first stop. He wanted to introduce her to his world, to show her that it was as purposeful as hers, and that it just had more trimmings. No woman had ever made him feel the need to justify his wealth. Because they took it for granted, he concluded as he led the way to the lower deck. Jess took nothing for granted.

'This is incredible,' she breathed as she stared with interest at his state-of-the-art equine facility. 'I'm even more impressed than I was on the upper deck. 'You've thought of absolutely everything.'

'Horses are my life,' he confessed, dragging deep on the familiar and much-loved scent of warm horse and clean leather.

'Do you mind if I stay down here while we take off? I'm concerned that the noise might spook Moon.'

'The pilot won't allow you to wander around at will. You'll have to be strapped in for take-off. The grooms have their own drop-down seats, much like the cabin attendants on a regular flight.'

'So long as Moon knows I'm here,' she agreed. 'Why don't you go back upstairs and relax? There's no reason for both of us to be here. I'm sure the grooms and I can handle everything. Why don't you take the chance to rest that leg?'

'I'm not an invalid,' he retorted sharply.

'No. You're anything you choose to be,' Jess agreed with a pointed look at his cane.

'I hope you're not suggesting that it's my choice to use this?'

'You don't have much alternative at the moment,' she pointed out. 'Nor will you until you accept treatment.'

'I'll be staying down here too,' he gritted out, keen

to change the subject. 'These ponies represent a huge financial outlay—'

'Don't give me that,' she flashed back. 'You love them as much as I do.'

'I care for all my animals,' he conceded, 'and I've noticed, as you must have done, that Moon is particularly edgy, so I'll be staying with her when we take off.'

'One rule for you and another for me?' Jess challenged. 'Don't *you* have to be strapped in?'

'It's my jet and I do what the hell I like.'

'Regardless of safety?'

'Don't make me send you upstairs.'

'Why don't we both stay with Moon to reassure her?' she suggested mildly, refusing to rise to his threat.

'Because spending time with a woman who appears to take pleasure in sticking sharp words into my leg and shattering glances at my cane holds zero appeal.'

'Oh, I think you can take it,' she said. 'As you must shortly take some painful treatment.'

'You know a lot about me. Or think you do.'

Jess ignored this too and as she slipped into Moon's stall he followed her.

Moon became agitated when the jet engines screamed, eyes rolling back in her head.

They stood either side of the anxious mare to soothe her. Perhaps the combination of two people who cared got through to the spooked animal. Moon settled and allowed him to scratch a favoured spot beneath her chin. By the time the jet had levelled out everything was calm again. Which was why Jess's tense expression surprised him.

'You okay?' he asked.

'Of course.'

He was going home, but Jess was taking a step into the unknown, he reasoned as she worried her bottom lip.

'You've been standing long enough,' she said, switching the spotlight to him.

Who was in charge here? His concern for Jess evaporated. 'You don't give orders on my flight.'

'Agreed,' she said without objection.

'But?'

She braced herself as if preparing to drop a bombshell.

'Spit it out,' he advised.

'You're in my care.'

'I'm sorry?' he queried, frowning.

'This is as good a time as any to explain that your siblings hired me to treat your leg. Which means obeying my instructions,' she went on before he could answer. 'The alternative is to throw their care and love for you back in their faces.'

'How long have you known this?' he asked in an ominously measured tone.

'I swear I haven't had chance to tell you before now. Yesterday flew by—'

'And you could not have made time?' he queried, controlling everything in his manner and voice to avoid upsetting the skittish mare.

'I didn't want anything to worry my father.'

'And how would this news have done that? Surely he'd be glad you've got another high-profile client?'

'All right,' she admitted. 'I anticipated your reaction, and I'm worried about you. You need this treatment badly, so please don't be angry. I'm very good at what I do. Your brothers and sister wouldn't have hired me otherwise.'

He shook his head. 'You should have told me at the first opportunity.'

'And I have.' She held his stare without blinking. 'You can always refuse treatment, but for your sake I hope you don't.'

Truth might be blazing from Jess's eyes, but that wasn't enough to stop him feeling deceived and wrong-footed. 'We'll pick this up another time.'

'This is surely not a complete shock. You knew you would be undergoing treatment.'

'Not with you. I was expecting a physiotherapist, yes.'

'And you've got one,' Jess pointed out. 'One with three years' experience at a prestigious London teaching hospital before I went into private practice to allow for more flexibility.'

So she could take care of her father, he presumed Jess meant by that. He couldn't knock her for something he would have done. Family meant everything to both of them.

'I'm known for my good results if people listen to me,' she went on. 'That's why your family contacted me. Word of mouth is the most effective marketing tool.'

He didn't trust himself to discuss this yet, and Moon, sensing discord between them, was fast becoming restless.

'You're unsettling her,' Jess murmured as if he needed this pointing out.

'Is that why you chose to tell me here? Because I couldn't make a fuss.'

'I think you'd better leave,' Jess told him in the same calm tone.

'No one tells me to leave.'

'It's best for the horse.'

'And you,' he pointed out with a sceptical huff. 'You go. I'll take care of Moon. She should know me. You can't cling to her for ever. It isn't fair to the horse. Go,' he instructed Jess as the pony grew increasingly agitated. 'If you love her, you'll entrust her to me.'

Jess's eyes were wide, and threatened tears. 'You'll take good care of her, won't you?'

'The well-being of my animals is paramount.'

'Just one more thing,' she said, and Dante paused for a moment. 'What would you have said if I had introduced myself as your therapist in the first place?'

Based on ten-year-old memories? He would have laughed her out of the room.

'Don't be angry with your family for caring about you,' she said as if reading his mind. 'I'm the best chance of recovery you've got.'

'We'll see, won't we?'

Swinging around, he turned his attention to the horse. The mare was soon quiet again. Moon trusted him instinctively. What she didn't like was friction between him and Jess. 'We'll have to do something about that, won't we?' he murmured in one silken ear.

Moon rewarded him immediately by calmly resting her head on his shoulder and whickering softly, as if to say yes.

CHAPTER FIVE

PERCHED TENSELY ON the edge of a deeply upholstered seat in the lounge area of Dante's super-jet, Jess brooded on whether she should have blurted out sooner, *I'm your therapist. I've been booked by your brothers and sister. Suck it up.* Well, maybe not that last—

'Are you sure you won't have another sparkling water, *señorita*?'

'No, thank you.' Suddenly aware of the empty glass she was nursing, Jess handed it over with a smile. The cabin attendants couldn't have been more helpful. Her surroundings were beyond impressive, from the plush leather and polished wood to the space. There was just so much space. She definitely wasn't used to that in the cheap seats. The interior of Dante's jet was more impressive than a mansion in a magazine. All light and bright and pristine, everything was of the highest quality.

Dante's expression could be described as anything but light and bright when she'd left him on the lower deck; trust was crucial between a therapist and their patient. Had she sacrificed that? Heaving a sigh, she won-

dered when she could have told him. Things had moved
so fast, because that was what her father wanted.

She could have made time.

Maybe, but that might have spoiled yesterday for
her father. And, selfishly, she had wanted time to get
to know Dante, and hadn't wanted to put a spike in
that either.

And now? What did she want now?

To get through this, and for Dante to accept treatment.

He was perfectly entitled to send her home.

What would be the point in that? Why delay his recovery when he had a therapist on hand? She would be
on the *estancia* to see the horses settled, so he might
as well accept treatment. Even Dante Acosta wasn't
superhuman.

*He just looked that way...smelled that way...acted
that way—*

'Excuse me, *señorita*...?'

It was the cabin attendant again. Jess looked up and
smiled. 'Yes?'

'Señor Acosta is waiting in the dining room.'

'I'll be right there.'

Jess's mouth dried. Did Dante's summons herald
a reprieve, or was she about to receive her marching
orders? Pausing only to smooth her hair and firm her
jaw, she set off to confront the wolf in his lair.

Dante had seated himself at the head of a full-sized
dining table, where he was ravenously devouring a
baguette and cheese. When Jess walked in he looked

up briefly. Indicating 'Sit' with a jerk of his chin, he swiped a linen napkin across his mouth. 'Are you hungry?'

'A little,' she admitted.

The look Jess was giving him suggested she couldn't deal with so much charm. Tough. He wasn't about to sugar-coat his manner for someone who had kept vital information from him.

'Eat,' he rapped, 'and then we'll talk.'

'That sounds ominous.'

Ignoring her comment, he finished his food and swilled it down with a large glass of water.

Jess made no attempt to take anything from the laden platters in front of her. 'Do you want something else?' he probed, frowning. 'If you do, ask.'

She looked uncomfortable. 'I don't want to put anyone to any trouble.'

'Really?' he said, sitting back. Keeping his stare fixed on Jess, he waved the attendants away and reached for some fruit.

'I'm not here to eat,' she insisted. 'You wanted to talk to me.'

He shrugged.

'You think I've taken advantage,' she stated tensely.

'That's exactly what I think,' he agreed.

'I'm sorry you feel that way.'

He held up a hand. 'Don't be. We're not so different, you and I. Why shouldn't you seize an opportunity? I would have done exactly the same thing.'

Her frown deepened. 'So...?'

'So we're complicated.' Easing his shoulders, he

stared at her. 'Do I have to put something on a plate and feed you myself?'

Her eyes darkened. 'No, I'm—'

'Fine?' he suggested.

'Yes.'

'Relax, Jess. I have the greatest admiration for the caring profession. You should have told me from the start, but it's done. You're here. Now you have to put your manner of telling me behind you, as I do.'

'I didn't mean to deceive you. I just want to help.'

'My leg's aching,' he admitted. 'Why shouldn't you help? Grapes and cheese?'

She looked bemused for a moment, but then she relaxed. 'Thank you. I am hungry, and that would be good. I know I haven't made the best of starts, but I will make up for it.'

She certainly would, he thought.

The cheese was delicious and Dante was too. He was such a distraction she had trouble remembering important things, like why she was here and what she had come to do. He'd showered and his hair was still damp. It curled in thick black whorls that caught on his stubble. His earring glinted in the overhead lights, while the scent of lemons and something woody surrounded him. On home territory Dante was relaxed, wearing just a loosely belted robe after his shower. When he moved she caught glimpses of his tattoos... an edge of the snarling wolf across his heart and, when he turned to pour another glass of water, a glimpse of the skull and cross mallets tattooed across the back of his neck. How was she supposed to make easy conversation with all that going on?

'Eat up—take more,' he insisted. 'From what you've told me, I'll be working you hard.'

Jess's throat tightened. Shouldn't it be the other way around?

'If my treatment can't wait, I'm sure you're eager to begin,' he suggested dryly, with a long amused yet challenging look.

'Yes, of course,' she agreed in a voice turned dry.

'You have access to my medical history?'

'Scans, X-rays and a full set of notes,' she confirmed.

'Then there's no reason why you can't start right away. We're not going anywhere until this aircraft lands, so you might as well make a start. As you can see,' he added lazily, playing her like a minnow on the end of his rod, 'I dressed with that in mind.'

The thought of laying hands on Dante's body sent Jess's heart into a spin. Would she ever be ready to do that? She was a professional, with a job to do. Of course she could do it.

'I'm happy to start your treatment right now,' she said evenly.

It wasn't just Dante's sporting future she was holding in the palm of her hand, Jess realised. She wasn't so naïve that she didn't understand the boost her CV would receive if Dante's treatment resulted in him returning to world class polo.

'Second thoughts?' he suggested.

'None.'

'Then…' Dante was viewing her with amused eyes, as if he knew every thought in her head. 'You'll need a firm surface to work on, I presume?'

'Correct,' she confirmed.

'I'll make sure you have one. We will begin in half an hour.'

'That's good timing,' she agreed. 'You should digest your food first.'

'It will also give you chance to examine all the reasons you chose to come to Spain.'

'I have a contract,' she countered swiftly. 'And the lower deck of your aircraft is full of ponies that mean the world to me and my father.'

One of Dante's sweeping ebony brows lifted. 'You have an answer for everything, *señorita*. We will soon see if you have a solution for my damaged leg.'

Get over yourself, Dante mused as the minutes ticked slowly away. He shouldn't have allowed the situation to reach a point where his brothers and sister had been forced to intervene. But that was how the Acostas were. If one needed help and refused it, the others stepped in. Jess was stuck in the middle of a forceful, powerful family. He shouldn't be taking out his frustration on her. He'd been difficult since the polo accident. Hell, he'd always been difficult. He'd been the wayward son before his parents' death. It was only after the tragedy that he realised how much grief he'd given them. Now that grief was his. Verbal jousting with Jess had lifted him. He liked a challenge, and Jess was full of it. Without polo there was no conflict in his life. Jess gave him all he needed. Feeling her hands on his body was something he anticipated with interest.

'My bedroom?' he stated when she appeared at the appointed time.

'Perfect,' she agreed without batting an eyelid. 'We'll have privacy there.'

'So no one will hear me scream?' he suggested dryly.

'The treatment will be painful,' she admitted evenly, 'but I don't imagine you show your feelings as easily as that.'

They stared at each other for a moment. *Pot, kettle, black*, he thought, but at least Jess didn't shy away from her obligations. 'Lead the way,' she said pleasantly instead.

'I'm going to put a towel over you to preserve your modesty,' she told Dante in the reassuring tone she used with all her patients.

'What modesty?' he growled.

She blinked as she turned back to her patient and was confronted by an iron butt. Her heart thundered like crazy at the sight of something that would normally pass her by. A butt was a butt. They came in all shapes and sizes, and she had never judged anyone yet. Before now. In her defence, Dante had an exceptional butt. And the sooner she covered it with a towel the better.

His body was all over magnificent. Dante Acosta was as close to male perfection as it got.

'I'm ready,' he announced.

Are you? she felt like saying, but at least he'd bounced her out of the self-indulgent stare. Members of his crew had arranged a board on top of the bed and she'd added a cover on top so it was comfortable.

'Well?' he prompted. 'What are you waiting for?'

She would have to be made of stone not to appreciate the sight in front of her. 'I'll be starting on your calf and working up.'

'Great.'

'Don't get too excited. According to your notes, there's nothing wrong with your groin.'

'Very witty. I rather thought I would be staying here on my front anyway.'

'You will; don't worry,' she replied as she hauled his legs into a position to suit the upcoming therapy. 'Now lie still and don't move again. And please don't talk. We have less than an hour for this treatment, if you want to take a shower when I've finished.'

'What are you using?' Dante asked suspiciously as she slicked her hands with oil.

'Horse liniment. My bag's in the hold—'

'You're doing *what*?' he roared.

'Joke?' she said mildly, chalking one up for the therapist. 'This is straight out of your bathroom.'

'No more jokes,' Dante growled, which was her signal to dig deep into the muscles on his injured calf.

Applying her skill, she soon discovered the seat of the problem. Starting gently, she built up the pressure until Dante let rip with a violent curse.

'You're supposed to be curing me, not torturing me!'

'If you'd started treatment sooner your muscles wouldn't be in such a knot.'

'Then make allowances for that knot.'

'Stop deafening me. Stay still. Keep quiet,' she instructed. 'This will hurt if you don't submit—'

'*Submit?*' he roared, almost exploding off the bed.

She pressed her weight against his back…his warm, tanned, hard-muscled back. 'Lie back down,' she insisted.

'I could shake you off in an instant,' he warned.

'You could,' she agreed. 'But what good would that do? Meanwhile, I'm hearing your treatment time ticking away.'

'You're cool; I'll give you that,' he conceded.

Thank goodness that was how she appeared. It wasn't how she felt.

'Continue,' Dante instructed as he rested back on the bed. 'Though I imagine you're going to make me pay.'

An unseen smile hovered on her lips. 'Whatever makes you think that?'

'My infamous intuition,' Dante informed her.

He bit back a curse as Jess—or Skylar, as he preferred to think of her in this merciless mood—dug her fingers deep into a nerve.

'This is the price you pay for neglecting follow-up treatment,' she informed him when he snarled a complaint.

He didn't care for the tone of her voice.

'What do you think you're doing?' Jess demanded when he rolled off the bed.

'Getting a few things straight.'

'Like what?' she demanded, lifting her chin to confront him. But her glance dipped to his lips before it returned to his eyes.

They continued to stare at each other until her eyes sparkled and she couldn't hold back a laugh. He laughed too because this was real, this was Jess. She wouldn't have known how to flatter him if she'd tried.

'Down,' she instructed, pointing to the bed. 'I haven't finished with you yet. Take your treatment like a man.'

'With pleasure,' he agreed, smiling.

'There won't be too much of that,' she assured him.

'Pleasure?'

That one word was all he could get out before the torture began, but he had to confess that she was good by the end of the session. 'My leg feels a little easier,' he remarked with surprise.

'You'll pay for it tomorrow,' she predicted. 'One session isn't a cure. It's only the first step in a very long treatment.'

'Excellent.'

'Excellent? I can't promise to be gentle with you.'

'Please,' he said, staring into her eyes, 'don't hold back.' Jess was blushing deeply as he added, 'At least my siblings haven't wasted their money.'

'Wait—I want to check something before you go,' she said as he straightened up. With that, she knelt at his feet.

'You don't have to bow to me— *Mujer!*' he exclaimed

as she dug her fingers into an area he had so far treated with the care he might show an eggshell.

'There you go,' she announced with satisfaction. 'It is that muscle at the root of your problem.'

He had more muscles with more problems than she knew.

'And you had to prove it,' he observed as Jess stood up.

'Yes, of course I did. I know what I'm doing, you know.'

There was no doubt in his mind of that.

Something incredible had happened while all this was going on. The anger that had dogged him since the accident—an accident caused by his recklessness, as well as that of his opponent—evaporated and was replaced by good humour. Jess had released something in him. It was the same knack she'd had ten years ago when he was an over-confident youth of twenty-two. She could burst a bubble of entitlement with a flash of her emerald eyes. Maybe she had been in awe of the Acosta brothers when they strode into her father's stable, but she'd hidden it beneath a mix of teenage attitude—and one surprisingly bold action. She hadn't even been fazed by the little fluff-ball disgracing itself all over her clothes, or if she had, she hadn't shown it.

'Don't you see the funny side of this?' he enquired with interest. 'Teenage Jess turned regimental sergeant major where my treatment's concerned?'

'No, I don't,' she said flatly. 'Treating patients is a serious occupation for me. I don't find any of this amusing.'

'Liar,' he reprimanded her softly. 'You must be gloating deep down.'

Jess's expression remained unchanged.

Now the session had ended they went their separate ways, Jess to check on the horses, while he went to take a shower and get changed. Had he met his match? The thought that he might have done pleased him as he stared into the glass above the basin. Would she get the better of him? No. That would never happen and it was something Jess still had to learn.

But… As he eased his leg, and for the first time in a long time felt no pain, he thought his accusation of Jess gloating over her control of him had gone too far. Yes, she was in charge of his treatment; that was what she'd been hired to do. Early signs pointed to her therapy being effective. Instead of trying to wind her up, he should be thanking her. Jess was alone on new territory, where he controlled everything outside Jess's treatment plan. A little humility on his part wouldn't go amiss.

CHAPTER SIX

'THANK YOU,' Jess whispered as she stroked Moon's ears. She loved the contrast between sharp-edged cartilage and sleek, velvety hair and, even more than that, she loved the communion between them. The healing power of animals could never be overestimated in Jess's opinion. She only had to be in the stall with Moon to know that this closeness between them was a gift, a space, a special place to be—it was a place where she could always see things clearly. Except for Dante.

All those years she'd dreamed about him, without making allowances for the man he would become. In her mind, Dante had remained the dangerously attractive youth who hovered unseen, and yet so forcibly present, over every relationship she'd ever had. How was she supposed to have a successful love life with Dante Acosta as her template?

That kiss hadn't stopped him when it came to relationships.

No. Far from it. Following Dante's career meant following a great many stories of his private life, which ran alongside his success, both in polo and the tech world. While she applauded his many triumphs, she was forced to see him dating, and that cut deep.

It still did.

It hadn't damaged the connection between them. That was real and strong, at least on Jess's part, but did Dante feel it too? He was impossible to read. Even blazingly alive in front of her rather than haunting her mind, Dante was as intangible as he had ever been.

Could there ever be anything between them?

'Look at the state of me,' she murmured as Moon nuzzled her neck. 'Does that seem likely when women across the world are hammering on Dante's door? Why waste my life on pointless dreaming?'

'So here you are—'

She jumped at the sound of Dante's voice.

'I knew I'd find you with the ponies.'

Her swift intake of breath must have betrayed the fact she'd been thinking about him. If that wasn't enough, her cheeks were blazing and her lips felt swollen, while her breasts were aching for his touch.

Dante appeared totally unaffected. Ditching his cane to come into the stall, he lounged back against the wall to inform her, 'Look, no stick. I'm cured. You can go home now.'

'By parachute?' she suggested.

He laughed, a flash of strong white teeth against his dark, swarthy face, which was the cue for heat to rush through her. If there was one thing more dangerous than a grim-faced Dante Acosta, it was this version. She couldn't resist this one at all.

She must, Jess reminded herself. Professionalism was paramount. 'It's too soon to discard your stick,' she observed. 'I've already warned you that you'll suffer tomorrow if you put too much stress on that leg. You could pay the price with a setback.'

Dante's answer was an easy shrug. 'Relax. I left my cane outside to avoid spooking Moon.'

'And you delight in teasing me. Don't forget that.'

Dante almost turned serious. 'I delight in the improvement I can feel in my leg. You can claim a miracle if you like.'

'I prefer to work steadily until I'm sure that any improvement is lasting. I don't throw up my hands and cheer at the first sign of change.'

'Tell me, how do you remain so controlled?'

'It counters your teasing,' she said honestly. 'As for miracles? All I see in your future is more therapy, hard work and pain.'

'Sounds irresistible.'

'I thought you'd prefer to hear the truth.'

'Did you?'

The look he gave her now made Jess's cheeks flare bright red, while her body responded with far too much enthusiasm. 'I take it you're here to see Moon?' she said in an attempt to distract both of them from the mounting tension.

'I'm here to see you also.'

'Oh?'

'There's something I forgot to say to you.'

'You're fired?' she suggested dryly.

'Now, why would I do that when I think we're making progress?' Dante viewed her steadily. 'Small steps,' he explained.

Was he still referring to his leg? 'Small steps,' she agreed.

'Truce?'

She tensed as he pulled away from the wall. As he came closer and his heat wrapped around her, Dante's energy pervaded the atmosphere.

'I just want to say thank you,' he soothed.

He dipped forward to brush a kiss against her cheek, but she turned her head at entirely the wrong moment and their lips met. It seemed like for ever, though it could have been no more than a heartbeat, that she didn't move, breathe or register anything apart from the fact that Dante was kissing her and seemed in no hurry to move away.

'You okay?' he prompted, pulling back.

The penny dropped. No wonder he was frowning. In Dante's sophisticated world kisses were exchanged as easily as handshakes. 'Of course I'm okay.' She shrugged as if men like Dante Acosta kissed her every day of the week, when what she really wanted was for him to kiss her as if he really, *really* meant it. 'There's no need to thank me. It's my job.'

'You're very good at your job,' he observed in a tone that bore out every thought she had about the meaning of that kiss. There was no meaning beyond *Thank you*.

'And now it's time to strap in for landing,' he added briskly.

You can say that again, Jess thought, curbing misplaced amusement as Dante's dark stare lingered on her face.

'Now?' he prompted. 'We'll be touching down in a few minutes.'

His wake-up call was badly needed. She wasn't his type. If his perfunctory kiss hadn't proved it, any magazine in the world would show that Dante went for glamorous women, more at home on the front row of a high fashion show than the back row of the stalls.

Heading off to find a seat to strap into, she was surprised when Dante did the same. She'd already decided to stay on the deck with the horses so she was ready to help the grooms as soon as the plane landed. 'Why don't you strap in upstairs?' she suggested to Dante. 'We can manage here, and if you don't rest after treatment you'll never get better.'

'If you don't learn that I don't accept orders you and I are in for a bumpy ride,' he shot back.

Pressing her lips together so she didn't say something she might regret, Jess reflected tensely, *You don't frighten me, Dante Acosta, and, whether you like it or not, for the duration of your treatment I'm in charge.*

With the horses safely arrived in Spain and loaded into transporters waiting on the tarmac, it was Jess's turn to climb into Dante's flatbed alongside.

Flinging his cane into the back, Dante hauled himself into the driving seat beside her. 'You'll be in pain for some time yet,' she explained when he grimaced and paused to knead a cramped muscle. 'I dare say I've woken up nerve endings you'd forgotten about.'

'No chance of that now,' he agreed grimly. 'How long must I suffer cramp?'

'Until you're cured.'

'Then you'd better get on with it.'

'I intend to.'

As Dante shook his head with exasperation, Jess knew she was dealing with a warrior, a man who had thought himself invincible until the accident.

'You'd better make sure I'm ready for the new polo season,' he threatened, grimacing.

'I'd be lying if I said I could guarantee that. It's largely up to you, and how seriously you take my treatment plan.'

'Do you have to be so honest?'

'Always.'

'I can hire a therapist any day of the week.'

'Then go ahead and do so, though I can't imagine you'll have many takers if that expression settles on your face.'

'*Ha!* And what about the ponies? Or have you forgotten about them?'

'I've forgotten nothing,' she fired back. 'I'll stay on your *estancia* until they're settled, but that doesn't mean you have to keep me on as your therapist. Go ahead and hire someone else.' *At least I wouldn't have to tolerate you as a patient*, she thought, though deep down she knew it was the frustration of Dante's injury driving him to lash out at her. Better he did that than he took it out on someone who didn't understand him. 'I'm here to help and until you fire me that's what I'm going to do.'

'So you can put Acosta on your CV?' he suggested with an ugly snarl.

'So you can walk without a cane, and ride again, and maybe even play polo at international level again,' she argued calmly.

'Only maybe?' he said with a narrow-eyed look.

'There are no guarantees where the body is concerned,' she said honestly, 'but I've never shirked in my attempt to heal a patient yet, and I don't intend to start with you. I'm not a quitter, Dante.'

'Just my bad luck,' Dante murmured beneath his breath. Releasing the handbrake, he gunned the engine and they were off to a future even Skylar would find hard to predict.

While they were driving, Jess called her father to reassure him they'd landed safely and the horses had been loaded successfully without drama and were now on their way to Dante's ranch in Spain. It would have been a lie to add that things were going well, she reflected, and so she confined herself in a very British way to talking about the weather. 'It's warmer here in winter than Yorkshire in summer,' she told her father with a laugh.

'You enjoy yourself,' he said before cutting the line. 'All work and no play et cetera.'

'Thanks, Dad, I'll remember that.'

Dante glanced at her as they ended the conversation and she huffed a rueful laugh. 'Everything okay?' he asked.

'My father seems fine—on top of the world, in fact. I've never heard him sounding quite so optimistic.'

'Good. That's good.'

They both fell silent and she tried to relax, but it wasn't easy when she was trapped in the confines of a cab with so much man. Dante's lean tanned hands effortlessly tickling the wheel while his biceps bulged and his iron-hard thighs rested a hair's breadth away from hers would have tested the endurance of a saint. His machismo was like a living thing that sucked the air from her lungs, leaving her nothing to breathe but pure sex.

'I'm fast but safe,' he stated.

She laughed inside, wondering if she should feel quite so disappointed about the fast reference in that statement.

'You drive very well,' she said in an attempt to blank images of her life becoming fast and extremely unsafe. Her body wanted one thing, while common sense dictated caution. Twenty-seven years old and she couldn't boast a single successful sexual relationship, and that was all down to one man setting the bar at an unattainable height. Dante hadn't made things better with his most recent kiss. Even if it was just a token to say thank you, she was still buzzing with awareness and kept touching her lips with the tip of her tongue, as if to recreate the moment.

Okay, so she had been one hundred per cent guilty of sabotaging any potential love affair in the past by picking unworthy men. She didn't have time for love, she'd tell herself as she concentrated on her studies. Though she did have time to dream about Dante Acosta. And the failed love affairs? Were down to not wanting to tarnish that first romantic image of a memorable kiss in a stable. And who could blame her, when even a routine 'thank you' kiss from Dante Acosta set her heart pounding? He knocked the competition out of the park.

But there was no point in falling for a lost cause. She had to find a way to get him out of her system, or she'd never move forward and have the chance to love.

Not that she was in danger of falling in love with Dante Acosta. No way! Jess assured herself in the most forceful manner possible. Sucking in a deep breath, she made herself relax.

They'd been driving for around an hour when Dante announced, 'We're here.'

Anything Jess had imagined was obliterated by what she saw in front of her. Having left the bustling coast behind, the peace of this much lusher, greener interior held immediate appeal for Jess. 'How lucky you are,' she murmured as high gates swung back to reveal a crown of snow-capped mountains circling Dante's land. Neatly fenced paddocks full of ponies stretched away as far as the eye could see.

'I can ski in the morning and swim in the sea in the afternoon,' he said as they passed through the gates and drove on down an immaculately maintained road.

Lush green was fed by a glittering river, while clusters of trees provided shelter for the ponies. Jess was rendered speechless, and wondered how Dante could ever bring himself to leave.

'I spoke with my brother while you were busy with Moon. He says they booked you for a month.'

'I can't predict how long your treatment will take, but I would expect a substantial improvement by then.'

Dante hummed, leaving Jess to wonder if, for him, a month was too long or not long enough. Either way, she must separate her personal feelings from what she'd been tasked to do.

Each bend in the road revealed a new vista of contented animals and tidily maintained land. 'I've never seen so many ponies in one place before,' Jess admitted on an incredulous laugh, 'but what about security?'

'High-tech.'

Like everything else in Dante's life, she imagined. 'You've got a lot of plates to keep spinning, and once you return to full fitness I suspect you'll want to spin even more. Do you ever take a break?'

'Do you?' he countered with a swift sideways glance.

They fell silent after that, which allowed Jess to appreciate how big his ranch was. It was like a small country within a country, and when she contrasted that with the small hill farm where she'd grown up she got an even greater sense of the yawning gulf between them.

'Do you like what you see?' Dante enquired.

'The more I see, the more I understand why you chose to come here to lick your wounds.'

'It's my home,' he said, as if this were obvious.

But it was more than that, Jess suspected. This was Dante's retreat from the world, where he could live free from comment or the cruel gossip that suggested he might never play again. That gossip made her doubly determined to heal him.

Though there might be more to heal than Dante's leg, she accepted. He was a complex man who had famously run wild in his youth, only to be drawn to a shuddering halt by the death of his parents. Since then, it was well documented that Dante had done everything he could to help his oldest brother take care of the family. That took its toll as well, she reflected, thinking of her father's distressing retreat from the world when he'd lost his wife. Nothing hurt more than seeing someone she loved suffering as much as her father had, and Dante had gone through that same torment with his brothers and sister, which made her wonder how much time he'd taken to grieve.

'Another couple of miles and you'll be able to see all the facilities, as well as the ranch house and the stables.'

Meanwhile, she would feast her eyes on Dante's hands, lightly controlling the wheel, and his powerful forearms, shaded with just the right amount of dark hair.

Another couple of miles?

Could she control her breathing for that long?

She must, and she would. It wasn't a gulf between them; it was an ocean. She had entered a kingdom for one, which would be forced in the short term to play host to an invader with a medical bag.

And a will every bit as strong as Dante Acosta's.

CHAPTER SEVEN

'MY FATHER TAUGHT me that the handing over process is as important as the sale, so I'll see the ponies settled in before I go to my accommodation, if that's okay with you?' Jess said as Dante drew into a courtyard the size of a couple of football pitches.

'Don't worry. Your father's ponies have come to the best home in Spain.'

'I can imagine,' she agreed, 'but I promised that I would see them settled, and then ring to reassure him. After that, I'll concentrate on you.'

'That sounds ominous,' Dante said as he rested his hands on the wheel.

'You're my patient, and that makes you my primary concern.'

'I'm very glad to hear it.'

The way he spoke, the way he looked at her, was going to make it hard to remain immune to the infamous Acosta charm.

Make that impossible, Jess thought as Dante climbed down from the driver's side and came around the vehicle to help her out.

'I can manage, thank you.'

Ignoring her comment, he lifted her down, leaving her with the overwhelming and inconvenient urge to be naked with him, skin to heated skin.

'When you've reassured yourself regarding the ponies, my housekeeper will show you around the ranch house. Or you can sit on the fence and watch as I allow the ponies to stretch their legs. They've been cooped up and will appreciate some carefully controlled freedom.'

'Sit on the fence?' she queried wryly. 'Does that sound like me?'

'No,' Dante admitted, 'but the sooner the ponies get used to new handlers, the happier they will be.'

For a moment Jess felt excluded, and had to remind herself that interaction with her father's ponies was to reassure him and that her main job was to treat Dante.

But she couldn't help herself, and when she noticed Moon playing up she walked over to the wrangler. 'Let me do this,' she insisted as the tricky mare reared. 'I know Moon. I understand her.'

'*Está bien*, Manuel. Back off,' Dante instructed as Jess took charge.

The ease with which she was able to calm Moon was almost embarrassing. Everyone stopped to watch as she brought the pony down the yard but, not wanting to start off on the wrong foot, she explained to the assembled wranglers, while Dante translated her words from English to Spanish, that the mare trusted her because she'd known Jess since the day she was born.

'They appreciated that,' Dante remarked as he led

the way into the quarantine area where Moon would be allowed to roam.

'No problem. I know the ponies, and soon they will too. 'Treatment after supper,' she reminded him as they removed Moon's halter and set her free.

'I'm braced and ready,' Dante assured her dryly, 'but I'm handing you over to my housekeeper, Maria, while I catch up with what's been happening on the ranch.'

Maria gave Jess the warmest of welcomes, but even the most informative tour of the spacious and luxuriously appointed ranch house, with its burnished wood and richly coloured furnishings, failed to distract Jess from thoughts of Dante. She had to find a way to put him out of her mind. At least until his next treatment when, for a short time only, he would be the focus of her mind and not her heart, she determined.

'I see you've made yourself at home,' Dante commented later at supper. He had lined up in the cookhouse with everyone else, while Jess was behind the counter, serving with Maria and Manuel, the wrangler she'd met earlier.

'And what a home,' Jess commented, smiling as she handed over Dante's loaded plate. 'Maria invited me to throw myself in at the deep end, which was exactly what I wanted to do. So here I am.'

Dante glanced around. 'You approve?'

'Who wouldn't?' she enthused. Dante's ranch had an air of purpose and everything was of the highest quality, including the delicious food.

'You don't have to do this,' he said bluntly.

'But I want to. I'm not used to idling my time away.'

His eyes took on a darkly amused glint. 'I'm not enough for you?'

'Even with two therapy sessions a day, that's only a few hours of my time.'

With a shrug, he moved on and she attended to the line behind him.

When it came to Jess's turn to eat, there was one space left and Dante was sitting at the same table. It was a table for two, and their knees brushed when she sat down. An attempt to tuck her legs away failed. There just wasn't enough room. 'Sorry,' she said wryly.

'Too close to the fire?' Dante suggested.

'I can handle it,' she assured him.

'I'm sure you can,' he agreed.

Brooding and aloof was easier to deal with than a decidedly relaxed man, Jess reflected as she got stuck in to the spicy paella.

'One last check on the ponies and then I'll be ready for my treatment,' he said, pushing his plate away and standing up.

'I'll come with you.'

'As you wish.'

Dante stabbed his cane impatiently against the cobbles as they crossed the yard. She guessed his leg was giving him hell, as she had predicted. Her treatment on the plane had been deep and thorough. The memory of her hands on Dante's body made a frisson of anticipation rip down her spine at the thought of doing it again. Could she resist him for an entire month? Would Jess, the coolly professional therapist, do her work and go home, or would all that longing locked inside her break free at some point?

She could do this, she told herself as she followed Dante into the isolation block where her ponies would be kept until they had been checked over and passed fit by his veterinarians. The past had formed her and made her strong. The present brought new challenges, but so far she'd seen them through. There was no reason to suppose she'd falter now.

The facility resembled a top-class equine hotel. She turned full circle to take it in. 'This is wonderful.' Spotless surroundings, spacious stalls and animals contentedly resting was Jess's idea of heaven. She told him so.

'You can move in,' he offered, lips tugging in the hint of a smile.

'If I liked hay for a bed and oats for supper, I might just do that.' But she was laughing and relaxed; they both were.

His libido shot through the roof at the sound of Jess laughing, but his leg let him down by yowling on cue. He couldn't wait long for that treatment.

They checked each pony in turn. When Jess ran capable hands over them, murmuring soft words of encouragement, he craved the same attention. When they walked out of the stable block even the resident cats in the yard came to wind themselves around her legs. 'Next time I'll come prepared with treats,' Jess promised her feline admirers, kneeling down to give them a fuss.

'You have quite a menagerie,' she commented, smiling in welcome as one of his older dogs heaved itself up from its vantage point in front of the kitchen door. Animals were the best judge of character, he knew, and from then on Bouncer stuck close to her side as they completed the tour.

Several members of staff greeted Jess as if she'd lived on the *estancia* all her life. Light spilled onto her auburn hair in the veterinary hospital, setting it on fire as she chatted easily with his veterinarians in the sick bay. When they left the facility she reminded him he was due a treatment. 'Another session tonight, and then I'll leave you alone until tomorrow morning,' she promised.

Drawing her into the safety of the shadows as a truck loaded with sacks of feed trundled past, it was Jess who broke free first. 'Sorry,' she said as if she'd done something wrong.

He gave a relaxed shrug. 'Don't apologise.' He could get used to the feel of Jess beneath his hands. 'See you in half an hour for my treatment? Ask Maria to show you the way to the sports complex. There are treatment rooms there we can use.'

'Fine,' Jess confirmed. 'I'll do that.' But her emerald eyes were as dark as night and her tone was breathy.

Had that just happened? Almost happened. She was still tingling with awareness where Dante had held her out of the way of the truck. She had wanted to stay in his arms but couldn't do that and remain professional. This was only the start of her contract and she was already in danger of melting.

Entering the empty kitchen, she leaned back against the door and closed her eyes briefly. These might be fabulous surroundings and Dante was definitely the most attractive man she'd ever come across, but that was no excuse for her to lose her grip on reality. She couldn't afford to do that, even for a moment. She was here to treat a patient, and though the urge to continue what they'd started ten years ago—what *she* had started ten years ago—was overwhelming, it must remain locked in her mind. Maybe she would have to remain unsatisfied for the rest of her life, but better that than throw away everything she'd worked for on a dream that could never come true.

'Can I get you something, Señorita Slatehome?'

She jumped guiltily as Maria entered the kitchen. 'Jess. Please call me Jess.'

Quickly reorganising her features into those of a woman who hadn't been thinking heated thoughts, she smiled at Maria. 'I'm sorry to invade your beautiful kitchen, but Señor Acosta said you would be able to tell me where to find the sports complex.'

'He didn't have the patience to tell you himself?'

Maria's raisin-black eyes twinkled with laughter, as if this was the Señor Acosta she knew. 'You are a very welcome invasion, Señorita Jess, and I'm happy to direct you.'

But it was a struggle to concentrate when Maria began to explain. Jess felt as if her life had taken on a new and rapid speed and she had no way of slowing it down.

'If I can do anything else for you…' she realised Maria was saying.

'No, no, that's fine—to the side of the stable block, behind the yard—'

Maria laughed and corrected her indulgently. 'Señor Acosta is enough to make a saint lose concentration,' she reassured her.

'I'm hardly that,' Jess admitted.

'But you are a great improvement on previous visitors,' Maria told her with a significant look.

'Thank goodness for that.'

As they smiled at each other, Jess felt as if the bond that had formed the moment they met had tightened.

'Señorita Jess,' Maria added, catching hold of her before she left the kitchen, 'I would appreciate it if you could let me know if there's anything else you might need over the weekend, as I'm taking the day off on Saturday to start the preparations for my wedding.'

'Oh, how exciting!' And how good to have something to think about, apart from Dante. And a wedding was the best of all distractions.

'You're invited, of course,' Maria told her.

'Me?' Jess's hands flew to her chest.

'Of course you,' Maria confirmed. 'Everyone on the *estancia* is invited.'

Even Dante?

Jess's smile lost some of its sparkle. The less she saw of him in social situations, the better. Seeing him in the stable with horses was safe. Safe-ish, she amended. But weddings were emotionally charged affairs, infused with romantic overtones.

'Please say you'll accept,' Maria pressed. 'I think you'll enjoy it. I'm planning a traditional *gitanos* wedding with a Christmas theme. It will be held before Christmas in the marquee Señor Acosta has arranged here. He's so kind…so generous—'

So The Wolf had a heart after all, Jess reflected wryly as Maria continued to enthuse about Dante's many virtues. 'I'd be honoured to celebrate the day with you, Maria.' Whatever she thought of Dante, Jess wouldn't dream of offending her new friend, and the prospect of attending an authentic *gitanos* wedding was a bonus she had never expected. 'I'm really excited for you,' she admitted as she and Maria shared a hug. 'It's a privilege to be included in something so personal and romantic when I'm a newcomer to the ranch. Please let me know if I can do anything for you.'

'Just be happy here,' Maria implored her with a long thoughtful look as they released each other and stood back.

'Being welcomed like this, how could I not be happy?'

Dante. Wanting more than he could ever give her.

So, Jess reflected as she made her way to the sports building, twice daily physio sessions with Dante, and now a wedding. Was it even ethical to continue treating him, when all she could think about were the possibilities ahead?

These were early days, Jess reassured herself as the sports complex loomed in front of her. All stark steel and glass, it appeared more than fit for a billionaire's purpose. Which was more than could be said for her,

Jess concluded with amusement when she caught sight of her reflection in a sheet of glass. She doubted many of Dante's companions went to meet him dressed in scrubs and clogs, carrying a medical bag—unless he had kinks she didn't know about. This thought made her smile, made her determined to get used to seeing him, touching him. She would rein in her feelings. She had to.

But could she?

CHAPTER EIGHT

DANTE PICKED UP some calls while he waited for Jess in the sports block. Each supplied another small piece of the jigsaw that was Jess. He already knew she was a complicated woman, driven, successful and determined. She was also beautiful and he wanted her, but these shreds of information supplied by his team fleshed out the back-story of who she was.

He should have known the bold teenager would rise above the tragedy of losing her mother and develop into someone whose only thought was helping others. Competent and organised, Jess's reputation in her profession was second to none. But did he want to get close to her? Did he want to get close to anyone? The loss of his parents had been unbearable. Grief had frozen his heart.

With nothing but his racing thoughts for company, he soon became impatient. Before the accident he'd had many outlets for his energy: riding horses, women, working out in the gym. That appetite was only slumbering. Flexing his muscles, he turned on his stomach to rest his face on folded arms. Closing his eyes, he breathed steadily and deeply in an attempt to block Jess out, and then flinched, feeling her cool hands on his skin.

'Apologies,' she said in her best no-nonsense voice. 'Are my hands too cold for you?'

'You'll soon warm up,' he predicted.

Telling his body to behave was unnecessary when she began work on his muscles. *'Infierno sangriento!* Hold off!' he warned as she delved into the site of his injury with all the finesse of a commando in the gym.

'I know what I'm doing.'

And with that she put the flat of her hands between his shoulder blades and shoved him down again. 'Don't worry,' she soothed. 'This will soon be over.'

More accustomed to caresses and hungry, urging grips, he growled a soft warning as she kneaded and probed his tender damaged leg.

'Try to relax,' she insisted.

'Are you enjoying this?'

'It's my job.'

'Then improve your bedside manner,' he rapped, 'and while you're at it refine your touch.'

'It's my intention to heal, not pleasure.'

He huffed a cynical believing laugh.

'Settle down,' she instructed.

'Don't tell me what to do.'

'Are you going to take over the session?' She stood back.

'Get on with it,' he growled ungraciously.

'No more talking. Or laughing,' she added as he

shook his head and huffed with incredulity that he was still here, still tolerating her torture.

'You've got enough to think about,' Jess assured him. 'As I do, if these leg muscles are ever going to heal.' To prove her point, she applied even greater force to her pummelling and kneading.

'I'm not a lump of dough.'

'No. You're a lot noisier,' she observed. 'And far less pliable. So be quiet.'

'I could fire you.'

'Really?'

She sounded far too enthusiastic about that idea, so reluctantly he submitted, but not before he had acknowledged how quickly charming Jess could revert to Jess the therapist. That impressed him. In the ability to disconnect, she was very like him.

'If you don't obey my instructions,' she murmured as she worked, 'these sessions will be endless.'

'Really?'

'Stop that,' she warned in response to his amusement. 'Any slight improvement you've noticed after our session on the plane only signals the fact that certain muscles and nerve endings are being called into use again. That's a good sign, but it doesn't mean you're cured.'

He gritted his teeth as she gave him a good workout.

'Turn over. I need to work on the front of your leg,' she explained.

He couldn't turn over until his body took the hint. 'Give me a minute,' he ground out, before silently reciting the alphabet backwards.

'Maybe I can help you,' she suggested with concern.

She certainly could.

'Do you have cramp?'

He had something. The mother of all hard-ons meant taking longer than he'd thought. 'Don't touch me,' he warned when Jess attempted to turn him over. 'You might strain your back, and then what happens to my treatment?'

'I'm overwhelmed by your concern,' she murmured with a smile in her voice. 'But if you co-operate I won't need to strain my back.'

'Wait,' he insisted.

'As you please.'

She wouldn't sound so prim if she knew the extent of his problem. She was killing him in more ways than one.

At last he could turn over. 'Carry on.'

Dante had the most beautiful body she'd ever seen. How could she ignore that—ignore him? Patients were at their most vulnerable on the couch beneath her hands, and Dante was no exception. She wanted to heal him and she knew what to do. She also wanted to touch and pleasure him, but that was off the menu. Thankfully, he behaved himself for the rest of the session, which allowed her to concentrate on her work.

Most of the time.

'I'm done for today,' she announced as she satisfied herself that progress had been made.

'Exhausted?' Dante suggested, turning his head to look at her.

'It would take more than a single session with you to do that.'

'You sound very sure.'

His expression made her blush, made her smile… made her smile broaden. It was impossible not to find some humour in this situation, and it seemed the harder she tried to remain aloof from Dante, the harder fate worked to screw up her plan.

Trapped in the beam of very dangerous eyes, she said firmly, 'I'm done for today.'

'*Muchas gracias, señorita*,' Dante murmured as he rolled off the couch.

'Don't mention it,' Jess said politely as he straightened up and towered over her. 'It's what I do. First thing tomorrow morning, back here, around eight?'

'I'll be in town tomorrow,' Dante said flatly as he snatched up a robe.

'What about your treatment?'

'It will have to wait.'

'But I need to establish a routine.'

Dante grunted. Was this his way of dismissing her? Was she going to be ditched like the doctors in the hospital? Was he really going to risk his future mobility?

'You can't afford to miss a treatment.'

'You decide this?' he asked with a narrowing of his night-black eyes.

'Yes,' Jess said bluntly. 'I decide your treatment programme. You're not cured yet. If you have to go into town, I can start earlier. Name your time.'

'Six o'clock.'

He made it sound like a challenge. 'Earlier, if you like,' she suggested mildly.

'The time suits me.'

'Then it suits me too,' she said pleasantly, as she seriously considered stamping on Dante's one good foot.

Rewarded by a grunt of assent, Jess had to admit the banter and contest of wills between them was arousing. Dante was a patient like no other. And there was no law against dreaming. No code of ethics could find fault with that.

'Excellent,' she confirmed, turning to go. 'I look forward to seeing you in the morning.'

Delay was the servant of pleasure, Dante reminded himself grimly as he took note of the resolve in Jess's expression. Next stop the pool. He glared at the loathed cane, hating that he needed it to balance as he thrust his feet into sliders.

'You won't need that soon,' Jess called across on her way out.

He hated that she witnessed his plight. But Jess of all people was bound to, he accepted reluctantly. That was why she was here. His siblings would hear more of this. Why had they chosen this disturbingly beautiful woman on a mission, when a troll would have suited him better? Were Jess's soft hands even capable of delivering pleasure? He was beginning to doubt he would ever find out. And that was a first for Dante Acosta.

So. That went well, Jess reflected grimly.

Instead of blanking Dante's brazen sexual appeal,

she had thought of little else throughout that entire session. And now it was a struggle not to stare at him through the floor-to-ceiling windows as he sliced through the pool like the hottest thing in black swimming shorts. Even with one leg below par, Dante's body housed an immensely powerful engine. Massive shoulders, rippling muscles and those steel girder arms required supercharged apparatus to drive them on.

'Don't overdo it!' she yelled out as he performed a neat turn at speed. Maybe he heard, probably not, but she doubted he was in the mood to heed advice. There was only so much instruction Dante could take before needing to paddle his own canoe.

A wave of unaccustomed uncertainty washed over her. The prospect of curing him seemed more elusive than ever.

'On your head be it,' she muttered as she walked on. If this was the first day, it would be a long month.

A long month of reliving what had happened between them all those years ago, and wondering if it would ever happen again. She had never forgotten the feeling of his lips on hers at the farm and that brush of his mouth on the plane had only served to intensify her longing.

Get a hold of yourself, Jess; it's never going to happen. And you shouldn't want it to. The man is a nightmare. It would never work.

Look on the bright side, Jess decided as she headed to the kitchen for a snack. In just a few weeks' time there'd be a wedding and lots of new people to meet. She didn't have to spend time with Dante. She could skirt around him between treatments; she'd do it. There was no excuse not to work hard and enjoy herself while she was here.

He felt peckish after his swim. Having checked the new ponies for the last time that day, he headed back to the house to find Maria baking in the kitchen, with Jess clearing up. Jess tensed when he walked in.

Helping himself to a handful of Maria's delicious *churros,* he watched the two women, marvelling at the speed with which they'd formed an easy friendship. He took years to get the measure of a man, and had no reason to get to know women in any depth. Since being misled about his parents' condition at the hospital, he'd found it hard to trust anyone outside his immediate family and staff. Jess was in the group marked pending.

He still remembered the vultures swooping at his parents' funeral, and how he and his siblings had quite literally stood back to back to defend from their greedy demands. The general thought had been that young headstrong youths couldn't hope to take care of themselves, let alone handle a family fortune and land. The scavengers soon learned that the Acostas might have been headstrong at one time, but duty had changed them for good. Some, like Maria, said the change was for the better. Others said not. One thing was sure. No one crossed them.

'I'll miss this woman when she leaves,' Maria told him in Spanish, distracting him as she fondly squeezed Jess's arm.

He grunted a response. His leg twinged. He flexed it.

Jess noticed.

'Better or worse?' she enquired, brushing a loose strand of hair back from her face.

'I haven't decided yet.' If anyone could look sexier with flour on their nose he had yet to meet them.

'I think you're feeling an improvement.'

'Oh, do you?' he said, indicating her nose.

She swiped at it. 'Better?'

'I think I liked it better before.'

His reward was her paint-stripping look.

'Didn't I give you exercises to do?' she prompted. 'Why are you here?'

'I choose to be.'

Their eyes met in a combative glance, accompanied by a now familiar tug in his groin. Jess's eyes had darkened. She could act professional all she liked, but Jess was a woman too.

'If you will excuse me?' he said politely as he made for the door. There was no rush. She was here for a month, and it was no longer a question of *if* Jess would yield to the hunger inside her, but how long it would take.

Stabbing his cane into the long-suffering yard, he conceded that even after one day of treatment his leg was beginning to show faint signs of improvement. He'd probably be stiff tomorrow, as Jess had predicted, but as she was around to sort it he wasn't too concerned. Anticipating more banter between them, he smiled. There was only one problem. Celibacy didn't suit him.

He took out his frustration in the gym. Boxing shorts, boots, strapped wrists, bandaged knuckles and a bandana to keep the sweat out of his eyes. He gave the bag hell. Jess had stressed no violent exercise, but Jess wasn't here. to hell with the programme. She should have taken his frustration into account.

And now he was aroused. He stopped, swore and resumed his vicious pounding until the heavy bag almost swung off the hook. Pausing to stare in the mirror, a monster stared back: Dante Acosta in his most primal form. He checked his leg with a scowl. It was still attached to his body. That was good enough for him.

Muscles pumped, his body covered in ink, signalling his allegiance to team Lobos; there was nothing genteel about men who played polo at his level. Or the level at which he'd played before the accident, he grimly amended with an explosive curse. Retrieving the hated cane, he swung around to find Jess watching him. 'Yes?'

'I thought I told you not to exercise, apart from the regime I gave you. Did you forget, or do you still imagine you can go your own way?'

'As I did when I left hospital?' he suggested, easing his neck.

'Look where that got you,' Jess countered, hands on hips. 'You shouldn't be standing without a cane so soon, and you certainly shouldn't be putting so much pressure on your leg.'

'You put unnecessary pressure on my patience,' he snarled.

'So, get out? Leave me alone?' she suggested with a lift of her brow.

'You put the words into my mouth.'

He glared down. Jess lifted her chin. Daggers drawn, they stared at each other until he murmured, 'Well? Are you going to punish me?'

She shrugged. 'If I must, I will.' Her words were casual, but the sexual tension between them had soared. This wasn't Jess the therapist but Jess the sexually aware woman. Smiling faintly, he raised a brow and waited. Her blush deepened, as he knew it would, but that didn't stop her mouthing off. 'So the great Dante Acosta knows better than a trained professional?'

'I stand by all my decisions.'

'Stubbornness doesn't seem to have worked for you,' she observed coolly with a pointed look at his leg. Then her gaze tracked up to his half-naked torso. She studied the snarling wolf tattooed in all its dramatic splendour across his heart. 'If you care about your team at all, you should listen.'

'And obey?' he suggested with a tug of his mouth.

'If you don't co-operate you won't progress and I can't extend my contract.'

'Did I ask you to?'

'No,' she admitted. 'But you should know I'm very busy.'

'And likely to be more so,' he observed shrewdly, 'if you succeed in curing me.'

'True,' she admitted. 'But I do have other successes.'

'Or you wouldn't be here,' he pointed out.

'Don't mess up, Dante,' she warned. 'I really think we're getting somewhere with your leg.'

It was good to see her tiger claws. To walk again

without a limp, and play world class polo, was all he wanted, and Jess's expression was absolutely firm.

'What do you want from me, Jess?' he asked as he swung a towel around his neck. 'What do you really want? You could have refused to treat me—recommended someone else. I'm not easy, and that's putting it mildly. You must have known you were taking a chance on complications after our encounter all those years ago.'

'If by complications you mean that foolhardy kiss…'

He hadn't expected her to be so blunt.

'I've come a long way since then. I'm a lot older, and successful in my own right. I viewed the chance to work on your leg as an interesting and challenging opportunity. Curing you remains my aim. It's not such a coincidence that your family hired me, or that you saved my family farm by buying up the best of the breeding stock. The Acostas and Jim Slatehome have a history of trust that extends back a number of years. I'm part of that.'

'So your agreeing to treat me had nothing to do with money, publicity, sex or bragging rights?'

'Correct,' she said with a huff of disbelief. 'Wow,' she added. 'You really do have a high opinion of yourself. You're not my only celebrity client. And if I wanted sex it wouldn't be here, and it wouldn't be with you.'

'You sure about that?'

'Let's get one thing straight. My focus remains returning you to full fitness. I don't accept *if*, only when you are cured. You may not like my regime. You may not like me, but that's irrelevant because if you do as I suggest you will be cured, if a cure is at all possible.'

Jess was all heat and anger as she stared into his eyes, but then, as if she'd been clinging to the edge of a cliff with her fingertips, she exhaled and closed her eyes. The result should be inevitable. It might have been, had he been a different man.

CHAPTER NINE

HAD SHE REALLY been that close to falling under the notorious Acosta spell? Her body confirmed the lapse by softening and yearning.

Dante made it easy to snap out of the slip when he murmured, 'You think I want to kiss you now?'

'I'm just hoping and praying that you see sense.' They had to work together, and it was crucial for Dante's injury that there were no more interruptions in his treatment.

His harsh laugh suggested there was no warmth inside him, but they had both suffered loss and unimaginable grief, and that could so often lead to closing down feelings. She wasn't exactly a dab hand at showing emotion herself. Since her mother's death it had been a relief to lose herself in work, where caring for the individual was paramount, and personal feelings had no place. Dante was challenging her isolation, making Jess want things she had never believed possible, like learning to love and daring to show it, and having the courage to lay her heart on the line.

Maybe they could help each other.

In another universe, she concluded. One where she wasn't a medical professional treating a patient, and Dante actually wanted to lower the barricade he'd built around his heart.

She jerked to attention when he spoke. 'Tired?' she queried. 'I guess I'm running on fumes too. Could I join you in town tomorrow, though, after our morning session?'

'So you do need something from me,' he remarked dryly.

'Yes, I could do with some advice on what to buy Maria for her wedding. She's invited me. I don't have anything to wear, or a gift to give the bride.'

'You don't have to give her anything. You weren't to know about this. You've just arrived from England. I'm sure Maria doesn't expect a gift.'

'That's not the point. I wouldn't dream of turning up without something nice after all her kindness to me. And I can't go dressed like this…' Jess ran a hand down her scrubs. 'This is all I've got with me, apart from spare uniforms and gear for riding.'

Dante dismissed her concerns with a shrug. 'Order what you like and I'll pay for it. The gift too.'

'That's not how it works,' she informed him bluntly. 'I set my own budget. The gift for Maria must come from my pocket, not yours.'

Dante's impatience showed itself again. 'You wouldn't be borrowing anything from me. Just think of it as a bonus on your charges.'

'Your brothers and sister have already paid me.' *But not danger money*, Jess thought as Dante speared her with an impatient stare. He was wealth-blind, and didn't have a clue how patronising he sounded sometimes. 'If it's not convenient to take me into town, just say so. Maybe I can borrow a car or a bike?'

'A bike?' he queried. 'Why not take a horse? You could tether it to the nearest lamppost while you shop.'

'Is there a bus?'

'No,' he said flatly. 'We're deep in the countryside and the nearest town is around twenty miles away. Why the rush? Must you go tomorrow?'

'It seems like a good opportunity. I'd like to start looking for a gift sooner rather than later, so if I don't find anything tomorrow I can always try again.'

'Nothing daunts you, does it?' he remarked.

'You'd better hope not,' she countered.

'I'll take you into town. Get some sleep. We leave first thing.'

'After your treatment,' she reminded him.

'At seven we leave.'

'Deal,' she said happily. It would be tight, but she'd make it work.

The next morning's physio went without a hitch—when you were on the clock there was no time for banter. There would be chance for plenty of that on their journey into town, Jess anticipated as they set off, but she would confine herself to bland remarks and try not to look too hard at Dante.

The sparring didn't take long to start.

'You shop, and then I'll take you to lunch,' he stated.

'There's no need. I imagined you'd drop me—'

'Over a cliff?' he suggested.

'In town, close to the shops,' she said evenly, refusing to rise to the bait. 'And don't worry. I'll make my own way back. A taxi or something.'

'Am I driving too fast? Are you frightened?'

Not of his driving, though Dante's skilful handling of the low-slung muscle car as it blazed a trail down the tarmac was surely at the limit of what was possible. 'I'm not frightened of anything.'

'Except yourself,' Dante suggested as she remembered to release her fingers from the edge of the seat. 'Don't worry. I won't hold you to my schedule.'

'I'm not worried, but you really don't have to buy lunch. I'm not dressed for somewhere fancy.'

'Am I?'

She had vowed not to look at him, study him, drink him in, but Dante had just made that pledge impossible. Even in jeans and a form-fitting top, he could go anywhere and be treated royally. With a body made for sin and a face to launch a thousand fantasies, Dante's piratical good looks would open any door.

'Can I trust you not to get lost?' he said when they arrived in town. 'Or had I better show you around first?'

'I'm sure I can manage,' she said, holding up her phone. It was time to escape from temptation.

Unfolding his formidable frame with annoying ease from the confines of the vehicle, Dante swore, retrieved his cane and swore again. Then, with a jerk of his chin, he led the way. She maintained space between them, but the streets were crowded. There seemed to be some sort of festival going on.

'It's market day,' Dante explained. 'Anything goes. Any excuse for a party.'

Jess glanced down at herself self-consciously. She certainly wasn't dressed for a *fiesta*. She'd had a quick shower and changed her clothes after Dante's treatment session, but her hair remained tied back and she was still make-up-free. She yelped as he held her back as a motorbike with a youth on board roared past within inches of her toes. Dante's touch was like an incendiary device to her senses.

'Careful,' he advised. 'You must remember what it was like to be a teenager—wild, reckless, risk-taking?' Her cheeks burned up as he added, 'There'll be a lot of them around today.'

'They grow up,' she said tensely.

'Some of them very well,' he agreed with a long, steady look. 'What made you decide to be a physiotherapist?'

It was a relief to have a question to answer. 'I promised my mother I'd finish my studies, whatever happened. I always had an interest in sports-related injuries, and equine sports in particular. When she died it made sense to have regular money coming in. My father went to pieces. I could help him.'

'So you tore yourself in two, working in London and spending your spare time on the farm.'

'I was lucky to land such a prestigious job,' she argued. 'I didn't want to leave my father, but my friends in the village promised to keep an eye on him. We needed the money, and I'd promised my mother. We all do what we must.'

'Your father's very lucky.'

'And so am I,' Jess insisted. 'My father was the first to encourage me to take the post. He reminded me of my mother's wishes, saying they were as one in that, and he'd never forgive himself if I stayed in the village because of him.'

'He struggled that much alone that you would have needed to?'

Jess hesitated, but then drew herself up tall. She was so lovely, Dante reflected, and so very proud. 'He loved my mother very much. It was…hard. I guessed he was lonely, so I returned home permanently. If it hadn't been for the help of the local village, I don't know what we'd have done. While I was freelancing, one of our neighbours would make sure to keep him company, and somehow we made it work.'

'Did London fulfil your expectations? Do you want to go back?'

'To living in one room in someone else's house?' She laughed. 'Don't get me wrong—the job was brilliant. I learned so much and had the most wonderful colleagues. I made lots of friends…'

'I'm sure you did.' There was an edge to Dante's voice. What did he imagine she meant?

'The type of friends you share a pizza with, maybe pick up some restricted-view seats in the West End to see a show.'

'Sounds…'

'Interesting?' she suggested with a grin. 'You've

got no idea. It was fun and it was formative. You don't need money to enjoy life. And I appreciate the quiet of Yorkshire and the peace of your *estancia* so much more now. The calm certainty and trust in the eyes of the animals we both love is enough for me. And yes, London's hectic and crowded, but it's fabulous too. There's so much to see, and not all of it has to be paid for. I always think that people like me with hardly any money can have the very best of London at their fingertips.'

Dante frowned. 'How's that?'

'There are so many opportunities available if you search them out. Loads of places are free to visit. There are beautiful parks and glorious buildings, and the river—' Was she boring him with her ultimate guide to the simple life? Dante's life was so very far removed from Jess's experience, it was hard to tell.

But his life on the ranch was low-key.

True, she conceded.

'Anyway, enough about me. Why don't we turn the spotlight on you?'

'I'd have to want you to do that,' Dante pointed out, 'and I don't.'

Undaunted, Jess pressed on. 'I don't imagine you have to hunt for parking spaces, catch a bus or miss the last Tube home.'

'I do have a house in London,' he revealed, 'but that doesn't mean I wouldn't like to see your side of London one day.'

'I'd be a flat-out liar if I didn't admit I'd like to see yours,' Jess admitted on a laugh.

'Are we talking compromise?' Dante enquired with a frown.

His expression was more amused than disapproving. 'We're talking,' she conceded with a smile.

Dante's sideways look made heat rush through her. 'It must have been hard for you.'

'No harder than it is for other people. What's hard about working alongside people I really liked and admired or being taught the skills that allow me to help people like you? I count that as a real privilege.'

'A vocation?'

'If you like.'

'You must miss your colleagues now you're self-employed.'

'We keep in touch, and I meet new people all the time. My life is rich and varied, so please don't feel sorry for me.' *It's one heck of a sight better than your life in your grass-fed ivory tower*, Jess concluded. Dante's inactivity was obviously eating away at him. She didn't need to be a medical professional to see that.

'So why physiotherapy?'

'Why specialise? It seemed an obvious choice. I grew up in the horse world where, like any extreme sport, there's always a need for medical professionals on standby. My skills allow me to work close to the animals I love, with the people surrounding them.'

'An introduction from me into the world of top-class polo wouldn't hurt your career,' Dante stated bluntly.

'No, it wouldn't,' she agreed, 'but that's a very cynical view. This isn't about me; it's about you, and returning you to fitness. I don't know who's used you in the past, but please don't tar me with the same brush. What you see is what you get with me. Take it or leave it.'

'But there's another side to your character.'

'Skylar?' she queried, cocking her head to one side to smile up. 'That's just a childhood nickname.'

'That suits you,' he said.

'Sometimes,' she agreed, 'but a name doesn't change me.'

'Just how you act,' he suggested.

'In a fortune-telling tent, maybe,' Jess conceded, 'but doesn't everyone have two sides to their character—private and public?'

He stared at her long and hard.

'There are a lot of genuine people out there,' she insisted, feeling she was being judged. 'You don't have to look any further than your ranch.'

'I hand-pick my staff.'

'While I was foisted on you?' Jess suggested lightly, but Dante didn't answer.

They had reached the main square. Guessing he must be desperate to break free, she suggested a plan. 'Leave me here. I'll take a cab back to the ranch.'

'I have something to drop off at my lawyer's office. You can shop while I do that, then we'll eat and I'll drive you back.'

A restaurant was a public place. There was no harm in eating with a patient and if he caught up with her shopping, Dante could advise on what Maria might like.

'Okay. I'll see you around here,' she agreed. 'But please, no swanky eateries. I'm not dressed for it; I'd feel uncomfortable.'

'I've got a restaurant in mind,' he informed her. 'Don't worry; it's casual. I think you'll like it.'

Nothing like her local greasy spoon, she guessed, but anything was fine by her.

She stood to watch as Dante made his way across the square. Taller than most, he was a standout figure. It was impossible for him to pass unnoticed. Plenty of people recognised him, and some asked for a photograph with the famous polo star. Not once did he swerve their attention or pretend not to see his fans. Dante behaved at all times with unfailing courtesy, as if he had all the time in the world to stand and chat. What she'd seen of him so far suggested Dante could be brooding and difficult, but who could blame him when he was reliant on a cane? This was the true side of him, she suspected, and it was a side she longed to see more of.

Caught out, she gasped when he swung around and pointed to her. The man he was talking to joined his hands together and shook them in the air, as if to praise and congratulate Jess. *We're not there yet*, she wanted to say. *We're a long way off.* But Dante telling people she was helping him gave her a thrill of pleasure that had nothing to do with boosting her CV.

Dante was back from his appointment before she knew it. She'd been so busy scouring the market stalls for likely gifts and trinkets she'd lost track of time. 'You haven't been away long.'

'Long enough to do what I needed to. That guy in the square,' he added, neatly side-stepping any potential questions, 'used to work for me before he retired. He asked how I was getting on, so I told him you'd get me back in the game.'

'That is my aim.'

'If I do as you say?' Dante suggested, dipping his head to direct a stare into her eyes.

'That will be the day,' she observed good-humouredly. 'But you will improve immeasurably. I'll make sure of it.'

'For some reason,' Dante confessed, 'I believe you.'

Having steered her towards a cobbled passageway leading off the square, Dante ushered her through a stone archway leading into a modest courtyard. Decorated with simple clay pots overflowing with flowers, the quaint wrought iron tables and chairs made eating outside a real treat for Jess at this time of year. But, to her disappointment, the restaurant was full. 'We can go somewhere else,' she suggested with a rueful shrug.

Dante's answer was to put his hand in the small of her back and usher her forward to where a small, capable-looking woman, wearing a mob-cap-style chef's hat and a crisp white apron, was cooking up a storm on an outside grill.

Catching sight of them, she passed her dishes over to an assistant and bustled forward to greet them. 'Dante, mi amor! Cómo estás?'

Jess knew enough Spanish to understand that the chef was asking how Dante was getting on. Concern showed clearly in the woman's eyes. When she turned to shake hands with Jess, she clasped both of Jess's hands in hers when Dante explained that it was Jess

who was treating his leg. 'Your poor leg,' she exclaimed
in English for Jess's benefit. 'Still no improvement?'

'Some,' he said, 'according to Skylar here.'

'Skylar?' she queried, studying Jess. 'What an interesting name.'

'Chef Ana,' Dante explained, introducing them.

'It's more of a childhood nickname,' Jess explained
to the cheery-faced older woman, 'but Señor Acosta
likes to use it.'

'Does he now?' Chef Ana murmured. Her smile
broadened as she glanced between them.

'We're hungry,' Dante stated, as if eager to break
the spell.

'When are you not hungry?' Chef Ana commented
with a shrug. 'It will take all your skills to heal him,'
she added in a stage whisper to Jess, before adding in
a far more discreet tone when Dante had turned away
to greet the waiters he knew, 'Dante has wounds you
cannot see.'

'I know,' Jess whispered back.

The two women exchanged a lingering glance as a
table and chairs were hastily set up for Dante and Jess,
and then, with a squeeze of Jess's shoulder, Chef Ana
gave Jess one last smile and left them to it.

Chef Ana's food was absolutely delicious. Platters of
finger-food to share lightened the mood and made banter between Dante and Jess inevitable as they jousted
for the last morsel of deliciousness. By the time the
platters were empty all Jess's sensible resolutions had
floated away. Was it even possible to sit across from
Dante and not want their legs to touch or their fingers

to brush, or their glances to meet and hold? With his hunger satisfied, Dante was a different man. Easy and charming, he made Jess relax to the point where she really believed they were beginning to know each other. She couldn't find much that was sensible in that, but if she were sensible what was she doing here?

Leaning back in his seat, Dante stared as he stretched out his legs. Part of her could have stayed like this all day, but her sensible head won through. 'What time does the market pack up?'

'Is that a hint?' he enquired.

'Yes,' Jess admitted, digging in her bag for some high value notes. It might be a small, modest-looking restaurant, but the food was top-class and the prices reflected this.

'Put your money away,' Dante insisted, but on this occasion she was too fast for him.

'I prefer to be independent,' she reminded him as she handed her money over to a waiter. 'You gave me a lift into town, so I pay for lunch. It's only fair.'

He seemed to find this amusing and exclaimed, '*Dios me salve de una mujer independiente!* God save me from an independent woman,' he translated when she gave him a look.

'You prefer a woman to be dependent?' It was a loaded question.

'Tell that to my sister and I'm a dead man,' he said. And Dante was smiling…laughing. 'I invited you to lunch, so I should pay.'

'Sounds to me as if you need more independent women in your life.'

'*Dios!* I have enough of them,' Dante exclaimed. Standing, he snatched up his cane. 'Okay, this is the deal. You pay for the meal, I pay for your dress.'

'Okay. But nothing fancy,' she insisted. 'And I buy Maria's wedding present with my own money. That's not up for discussion,' she added, 'though I would appreciate your advice as to what she might like.'

'We have a deal,' Dante confirmed.

This time Jess was sensible enough to nod rather than shake his hand and risk the consequences of touching him. 'I believe we do,' she agreed.

CHAPTER TEN

THE TOWN WAS more packed than ever by the time they left the restaurant. There were so many stalls she hadn't visited, Jess wasn't sure where to head first.

'Here,' Dante prompted, drawing her attention to a group of women on a stall full of beautifully crafted items.

She had set out to buy Maria's gift from what many would call a 'proper shop', but it soon became apparent that the items on the stall were unique. A tablecloth with drawn thread work was absolutely exquisite, but Jess doubted she could afford it. The cloth was so intricately worked the price would surely reflect the hours of dedication involved.

'Why don't we give it as a joint gift?' Dante suggested, seeing Jess's disappointment when she read the price tag.

'I couldn't do that,' she protested. Her mind raced as she considered how that might look.

'Why not?' he asked with a shrug.

She could give him a dozen good reasons. 'Don't worry; I'll find something else.'

'Here's another suggestion. Why don't I buy the cloth and you buy the napkins? You'd be helping me out,' Dante added. 'I don't have a clue what Maria might like, but I do know she loves to entertain, so this seems right to me.'

'And to me,' Jess agreed.

She loved the way Dante's mouth tugged up when he got his own way, but this suited her too, Jess reminded herself as they completed the transaction. She truly hoped Maria would love the tablecloth as much as Jess did.

More people recognised Dante as they left the stall. He stopped to chat, which gave Jess the chance to pick up some more things from neighbouring stalls.

'Have you found a dress?' he asked when the pack around him moved on.

'Not yet.'

'Follow me.'

How many times had he done this? she wondered before scolding herself for being so obviously jealous. Was it likely the type of glamorous women Dante was renowned for dating would pick out their clothes from a market stall?

He took her to what turned out to be the most popular outlet on the market. 'My sister loves this stall,' he explained, which put Jess firmly back in her box.

'Your sister has excellent taste.'

'Yes, she does. And I'm sure Skylar would approve.'

The clothes were certainly more colourful than Jess would usually choose, but no less attractive for that. There was no harm in combining Skylar and Jess for a harmless day out shopping, Jess decided. Her father sometimes accused her of not having a life outside work, and this was her chance to prove him wrong. She longed to try on something different, and Dante had predicted Skylar's taste to a tee. Her gaze did linger on a sensible mid-length tea dress, but that was definitely out of the running, she realised as Dante shook his head.

'You don't seriously expect me to wear one of these?' she protested when he handed over his selection. They were flirty and flimsy and quite definitely eye-catching, when Jess's preferred choice would suit a mouse.

His mother used to say he was an old soul, Dante remembered. He called it intuition. With no idea how he knew things in advance of them happening, he just accepted that he did. His gift was invaluable today when it came to choosing an outfit for Jess. 'We'll take the red dress,' he stated before Jess had chance to argue. That was the one she wanted. She could stare all she liked at the dull, sensible dress, but he wasn't buying it. As if to confirm his decision, her gaze strayed again to the racy red.

'Seriously?' she exclaimed. 'But that's the most expensive dress on the stall.'

'You want it, don't you?'

'What about this one?' she suggested, pointing to the dowdy offering she thought she should have.

'I'm not buying a dress for my grandmother.' And his decision was final.

The bright red dress with its spaghetti straps and a length barely south of decent was perfect for Jess, in his opinion. Handing over the cash, he ignored Jess's complaint that the dress was too short, too revealing, and that she'd probably catch a chill. 'This is the south of Spain, not the wild moors of Yorkshire,' he said as he pressed the package into her hands. 'And you want this one,' he pointed out with a shrug. 'Why pretend otherwise? We'll take the shawl too,' he told the stallholder, indicating an exquisitely worked length of smoke-grey lace. 'For decency's sake at the ceremony,' he explained to Jess. 'And for when it grows cool in the evening.'

'But the shawl's even more expensive than the dress,' she protested. 'I can't possibly accept these gifts when you've picked out the two priciest items on the stall.'

'You don't want them?' His expression remained deadpan.

'I can't accept them,' Jess insisted, tightening her lips.

'Hard luck. They're paid for. They're yours.'

'Ask for your money back,' she pleaded as he walked away. 'Please, Dante,' she begged, chasing after him. 'Don't embarrass me like this.'

'The stallholder's packing up.'

'Then catch her before she leaves!'

'So she loses the last sale of the day? Is that what you want?'

Jess deflated in front of his eyes. She was far too considerate to allow that to happen. 'Well, you shouldn't have done this,' she said with a shake of her head.

'I can. I did. And I should,' he argued. 'After all, you have to put up with me.'

'There is that,' she murmured dryly, 'though I'm determined to pay you back.'

As they passed the impromptu dance floor in the middle of the square, one of the local bands struck up. 'If you insist on paying me back, do so with a dance. It would be a great boost to my self-esteem.'

Like that needed a boost, he reflected with irony. 'It would prove your therapy's working.' True. It would also ease the ache in his groin. He had to put his hands on her soon, or he'd go mad. Delay might be the servant of pleasure, but it was also an aching test of his endurance.

'I can't dance,' Jess protested. 'I've got two left feet.'

'What about my self-esteem?' He delivered the words deadpan, with just the right edge of vulnerability in his tone to appeal to Jess's generous nature.

Her cheeks flushed pink. 'Put like that...'

'You can't refuse,' he confirmed.

'But just one dance,' Jess insisted with a concerned look in her eyes. 'You've been on your feet a lot today.'

He'd settle for that. 'I'll put your parcels behind the bar, and then we'll dance. If I feel the strain, I'll lean on you.'

He'd gone too far and she laughed. 'That'll be the day!' she exploded. 'But I do owe you for steering me towards such beautiful gifts.'

'That's right,' he confirmed, 'you do.' *Now, let's get on with it*, he silently urged. But his attitude towards Jess soon mellowed when he reviewed the sincerity in her eyes when she thanked him. Was he the first man to treat Jess as a woman should be treated? She should be spoiled. Jess had been working her ass off for years. What was wrong with cutting loose now and then?

'The dress wasn't a gift; it was a necessity,' he insisted. 'I brought you here—I landed you in this—'

'Fabulous and unexpected wedding invitation with a lovely new friend,' Jess interjected.

'Agreed. But you have to wear something at the wedding, apart from jodhpurs or scrubs.'

'True,' she conceded, smiling. 'And I'm thrilled to have such a pretty dress to wear at Maria's wedding, and I'm very grateful—'

'You don't have to be grateful. You've earned it. If there's a shortfall…' he pretended to ponder this '…I'll make sure you earn it. Does that salve your delicate conscience, and soothe your touchy pride?'

She shrugged ruefully. 'Whether I'll have the courage on the day to wear that particular dress remains to be seen,' she admitted with a grin. 'And I can't see it coming in handy at the farm.'

'Skylar would wear it,' he remarked.

'Yes, but she's a shameless hussy whose only skill is telling fortunes,' she dismissed.

'Can she dance?'

Jess's kissable lips pressed down as she considered this. 'Skylar can dance,' she confirmed.

'Just to be clear, when we hit the dance floor, am I dancing with Skylar or Jess?'

'Which would you prefer?'

'A freestyle combination of the two.'

'I'll have to see what we can do,' Jess offered with a grin.

'Knock yourself out.'

'I'll try to make things interesting,' she promised.

His lips curved. 'That's what I expect.'

But the best laid plans, et cetera, et cetera…

They'd barely reached the dance floor when his leg cramped. Seeing his grimace, Jess quickly reverted to professional in a trice and found him a seat. Kneeling on the cobbles in front of him, completely unconcerned by the people who had gathered to watch, she worked on the spasm, oblivious to everything but easing his pain.

Hell. This was not how he'd planned the evening to end.

'Better?' she asked, gazing up at him with concern.

'Much better,' he admitted in an ungracious low growl.

'No dancing for you,' she told him. 'It's time to go. That cramp was a warning. I'll get the rest of our things—' She handed him the cane.

He had never hated it more. 'I can manage without your assistance.'

Jess opened her mouth to reply, then thought better of it and stood back while he levered himself up.

They didn't speak a word for the first part of the journey home. He was in a foul mood, thanks to the cramp in his leg, and Jess had more sense than to attempt conversation. At least she showed more sense to begin with…

'You have to accept that your leg will take time to heal,' she ventured after they'd covered a few tense blocks. 'There will be setbacks, sometimes when you least expect them.'

'Thanks for the advice. Can we leave it now?' To emphasise the point he played some music. Jess talked over it.

'You're not invincible, Dante. You're a man, you're injured and you hurt. That isn't something to be embarrassed about.'

'Embarrassed?' he spat out with affront.

'If you tell me as soon as you get these cramps, maybe I can help.'

'Like you have done so far?' he derided.

'You're in pain now,' she intuited, 'so, rather than take it out on me, stop the car and let me drive.'

A short incredulous laugh shot out of him 'Are you serious?'

'Never more so,' she stated bluntly. 'It isn't a weakness to admit you need help. Open up. Trust someone—'

'Trust you?'

She blushed, but that didn't stop her asking, 'Why not? You have to start somewhere.'

'That's rich, coming from you, Jess. And no, you can't change places with me, either to drive this vehicle or to see things the way I do. So let's just agree to disagree and restrict our comments in future to subjects connected to my treatment.'

'Fine by me,' she bit out.

'Good.'

'Good,' she echoed before sinking back in her seat.

His mood didn't improve. If anything, it grew worse. If it hadn't been for the setback with his leg, he would

be planning to mark the successful business deal he'd
signed off at his lawyers round about now.

With Jess?

The connection between them was undeniable, but
they were worlds apart. She deserved more than he
could give—more than he wanted to give. Casual relationships suited him. His siblings were the one constant
in his life. He doubted he'd ever be tempted to extend
his family. After the tragedy of his parents' death, he
chose to fiercely protect what he had.

He glanced across at Jess. They couldn't avoid each
other. He needed more treatment, and they'd meet so-
cially at Maria's wedding, where he'd be polite, nothing
more. His world was constructed around practicality
with no space for pointless emotion. A good night's
sleep should sort him out, he reasoned as they hit the
highway and headed out of town. He'd attend Jess's
therapy sessions religiously, and he'd be civil when
they met away from the treatment couch, so when Jess's
contract ended he'd say goodbye without regret.

Jess felt the need to beat herself up. How could a day
that had started so well end so badly? She and Dante
were further apart than they had ever been, which
made it hard, if not impossible, to work with him. If
she didn't have Dante's trust she had nothing, and right
now the gulf between them felt wider than ever.

What more did she want?

To put it another way: what more could she expect?
Try nothing and she'd be close. Dante had spelled out

exactly what he wanted and expected of her, which was for Jess to heal him in the shortest time possible.

Frustrated by Dante's impatience, for which she had no answer, and by the black cloud surrounding them, Jess realised that she was gripping the packages they'd bought on the market as if they were comfort blankets. She desperately wanted Dante to be free from the shackles of his past. The loss of his parents was a scar he'd wear for ever, but would his parents have wanted him to pay a penance for their death every day of his life? She refused to believe it, but how could she help when Dante had shut her out? Perhaps he was right to do so and being professional from now on *was* the only way forward.

When Dante was under her hands on the treatment couch later that evening she marvelled at the miracle of healing. It had nothing to do with rich or poor, privileged or not, and had everything to do with training. Staring down at one of the most brutally physical men on the planet, currently resting on his stomach buck naked with the small exception of the towel she'd placed across his buttocks, she realised it was possible to separate her two selves and concentrate solely on healing. Manipulating his muscles until she felt the knots release was all the satisfaction she would ever need.

Was it? her cynical inner voice demanded.

It had to be.

'Well done,' she said, standing back when the session was over. 'That can't have been much fun.'

'Fun?' Turning over, he grimaced. 'If torture is fun, that was hilarious. You're a lot stronger than you look.'

Wasn't that the truth? Helping her father out of his financial difficulties was only half the story. When her mother died he took to drink, thinking this might numb the pain. But it was still there in the morning, only now he had a hangover to cope with, while Jess changed his sheets, washed his clothes and begged him to please take a shower. She suspected that these were secrets many other families were forced to keep.

As much as it had hurt like hell, the whole sorry experience had made her strong: physically strong as well as mentally robust. The first time she'd picked him up off the stairs, she'd strained her back. A refresher class in recovering unconscious patients from the floor had reminded her of techniques she should use to avoid injury. One step at a time, she'd told herself as she came to grips with caring for the broken man her father had become. 'One step at a time,' she'd whispered when he sobbed in her arms.

Now, thanks to the sale of the ponies, those dark nights were behind him and her father was back on top. He'd stopped drinking and took a shower every day. The washing machine went back to its regular cycle. Jess rejoiced to see him recover, but if she was totally honest she could see that being strong for her father had left her with no time to grieve. Just as well, she determined, firming her jaw. She had responsibilities, and a job to do, which she was good at.

What had caused the shadows in Jess's eyes? Dante reflected. Had someone hurt her?

Dante didn't invite questions into his life, and if Jess

wanted to tell him she would. He wasn't used to dealing with women who had so many onion skins to peel away before their true self was revealed, or maybe he'd never had the time or the inclination to do so before. Compared to Jess, those other women seemed like mannequins to him now. Jess was real—so real he missed the rapport they'd shared before their spat in the car. Their banter enlivened him, lifted him, and the pointless argument had been largely down to him and his frustration at not snapping back to full fitness immediately. That wasn't Jess's fault. She was doing her best to help.

'Don't rush off,' he said as she packed up her kit. Swinging off the couch, he tested his leg…not too bad. 'A lot of water has passed beneath the bridge since that kitten peed down your front, and you've shared so little with me.'

'While you've been incredibly forthcoming,' Jess observed dryly.

'Touché,' he conceded with a shrug and a smile. Then, after another few moments, he added, 'I apologise.'

That stopped her dead in her tracks. 'I'm sorry?'

'I was unreasonable in the car.'

'You were in pain.'

He didn't want understanding; he wanted a return to the up and down relationship they'd shared before. That was never boring. Professional civility was borderline. 'We can continue to snipe at each other or—'

'I must have stank in that stable,' she said, softening into the woman he wanted to know better. 'Belated apologies,' she added.

'For caring for a kitten?' He grinned. 'Apology unnecessary.'

'They were cute, weren't they...?'

She looked wistful as she thought back, no doubt remembering her mother alongside her in the barn, introducing her to the miracle of birth and teaching her how to care for kittens. How lovely she was.

'I have to go,' she said, breaking the spell. 'Apologies again, but I can't stay to chat. I promised Maria I'd call by to see if there's anything I can do to help with the wedding.'

'That's very kind of you.'

'I am kind.'

Yes, she was, and he'd almost lost her. Even now it was as if the connection between them had been reduced to the slimmest of threads. He wanted to kiss her, reassure her, and banish that sad look in her eyes, but not yet. This was not the time.

'Dante?' she queried. 'What are you thinking? You look so far away, yet so intense.'

He snapped to immediately. 'Just thinking about your charity event.'

'It was a good day, wasn't it?'

'A very good day. Successful, I hope?'

'Massively,' she admitted. 'Mostly thanks to you.'

He shrugged this off. 'It was your day. You organised it.' Jess was always thinking up ways to help others. Why hadn't someone helped Jess?

'The main thing to me is that it lifted my father.'

He nodded in agreement. Everyone in the horse world knew the saga of Jim Slatehome, and how the great man had been devastated by the death of his childhood sweetheart. When his wife had died Jim had gone to ground and hadn't been seen for several seasons. Surely someone must have noticed that Jess was reeling too? He guessed she'd put on a brave face because that was who she was. Her father had relied on her completely, and anything Jess had achieved personally, or for him, was a result of sheer willpower and grit. She didn't deserve to be abandoned now with no one to confide in.

'Three sessions tomorrow,' she reminded him brightly before she turned to go.

'Am I supposed to cheer?' he asked dryly.

'You're supposed to get up bright and early and set your mind to accepting three sessions a day from now on. If you attend each one and follow my exercise regime, I predict that in around a month you'll be back on your feet without that cane.'

His stare followed Jess as she walked away. There was such an air of purpose in her stride. He couldn't go right ahead and seduce her because Jess was special, unique, precious and oh, so tender beneath her onion skins of professionalism and grit. There weren't many he held in high regard outside his immediate family, but Jess Slatehome was right up there.

CHAPTER ELEVEN

A LOT COULD happen in a month. The run-up to Maria's wedding seemed to fly by. Jess had grown to feel at home on the ranch. In her free time she helped out wherever she could.

Dante had been as good as his word, attending each treatment session promptly, before fulfilling his quota of exercises as diligently as Jess could have wished for a patient.

She did a lot of wishing that month—that their banter could progress beyond amusing and superficial to something deeper, and that the man beneath her hands might somehow wake up one day to find her totally irresistible. This led to a lot of sleepless nights, but if she hoped for Dante to act on the ever-strengthening bond of friendship between them she was to be disappointed.

They learned more about each other for sure, but the facts remained these: Dante worked on his leg. She worked on him.

He rode more and more, which was amazing to see, while she made notes on his progress, revelled in his surprisingly wide-ranging library, walked the ranch, rode out on her own, which was what she was used to in Yorkshire, and spent time with Maria, who was the closest thing to a sister Jess had ever had.

And today was the morning of the wedding.

Jess stood, hand clasped to her mouth in shock, in the middle of Maria's cosy sitting room. 'Me? Be your bridesmaid? Are you serious?'

Jess was overwhelmed, while Maria was clearly embarrassed at having to ask Jess at the last moment to stand in for her one and only bridesmaid, who had gone down with a bad cold. 'It's such an honour! I can't believe it. Of course I'll hold your flowers at the crucial moment. I'll do anything I can. Are you sure? Isn't there anyone else you'd like to ask?'

Maria bit down on her lip. 'Can I be completely honest?'

'Of course,' Jess said warmly.

Pulling a face, Maria laughed and blushed. 'You're the only one who'll fit into the dress.'

Jess's peal of laughter set Maria off. 'I can't think of a better reason,' Jess admitted as the two women hugged.

'But the best reason of all,' Maria said in all seriousness when they parted, 'is that I like you and trust you to do this for me.'

'Then I'm honoured and thrilled to accept,' Jess confirmed. 'Do you think I should try on the dress, just to be sure it fits?'

'Of course…'

Crossing the room, Maria returned with a dream of a gown.

'This is so beautiful,' Jess breathed in awe. The delicate confection comprised of lace and tulle and was lovely enough for any bride to wear on her wedding day.

'I hope you like it?' Maria asked with concern.

'I love it.' Jess sighed as she stroked the peach lace and chiffon. 'I've never had the chance to wear anything like this.'

'Wait until you see my wedding dress,' Maria exclaimed happily. 'Señor Acosta insisted that the gowns came from Paris, so he flew me and my mother there, saying she must have a special outfit too.'

'He's very generous,' Jess murmured thoughtfully.

'Oh, yes, he is,' Maria enthused. 'Everything was handmade in the atelier of a very famous designer.'

'If only he weren't so obstinate and remote. If he just let people in and…' Her voice tailed away. Maria was looking at her as if she sympathised and yet wanted Jess to come to some conclusion by herself.

'I'm sorry,' Jess said gently. 'He's always been kind to both of us. I didn't mean to criticise him—especially not to you, and not on the morning of your wedding. How selfish you must think me.'

'Not at all.' Maria took Jess's hands in hers and held them tightly. 'Like you, he's hurt and scarred by loss and, like you, he says nothing. Both of you lose yourselves in work, and it's only this accident that forced Dante to pause and take a proper look around at things that matter. Like you—'

'Me?' Jess exclaimed incredulously.

'Can't you see it? Can't you see how much he needs

you—how much you need him? You complete each other. You're the missing parts to each other's heart. Perhaps I can see it clearly because I have The Sight, but you do too, don't you… Skylar?'

Jess smiled crookedly as she stared into the eyes of a woman she trusted like no other. 'Who told you my mother's name for me?'

'Dante. He doesn't open up very often, but when he does and I see the man behind the scars I love him like a brother. Neither of you is looking for pity, Jess, I know that, but what you should be looking for is love to fill the hollow in your heart.'

They hugged and then Maria whispered, 'Okay now?'

'Okay,' Jess confirmed, burying her face in Maria's shoulder. 'And so honoured that you've asked me to be part of your special day. Are you sure you trust me to wear this?' she asked as they broke apart and Maria took the beautiful gown she wanted Jess to wear off its hanger.

Jess viewed the intricately worked creation with awe. The beading was so delicate, and the cut of the gown so flattering it belonged in a costume museum rather than on the sturdy body of a hill farmer's daughter.

'Of course I'm sure,' Maria stated firmly. 'You'll look beautiful. Pale peach is the perfect foil for your fiery auburn hair.'

'I'll take good care of it,' Jess promised, vowing silently not to step on the hem and rip it, or snag the beading with her ragged nails.

As if reading her concerns, Maria added, 'Señor

Acosta has arranged a beautician and a hairdresser to attend me, and I hope you'll join in the fun. I'm guessing you're not used to that sort of thing any more than I am. It would give me confidence,' she insisted. 'Señor Acosta has made the premier guest suite on his *estancia* available for our use.'

'I… Oh…'

What was wrong with getting changed into a bridal outfit in Dante's house, apart from the fact that it was a reminder that Jess had no happy occasion on the horizon, or anywhere close, for that matter?

'It would really help me,' Maria said, having no doubt interpreted Jess's expression as stage fright. 'Neither of us is used to dressing up in such finery, but I'd feel so much better if you'd share this experience with me. I'd really value your honest opinion.'

'You can be sure of it,' Jess promised warmly. This was Maria's day and she'd give her all to it.

Dante had offered to act as father of the bride and give Maria away, but Maria had refused, saying she would walk herself down the aisle. Maria's attitude reminded him why he had hired her. No-nonsense and capable in so many ways, Maria, in turn, reminded him of Jess, a woman he confidently expected to appear at any moment, dressed in a provocative slip of a bright red dress. It was too late to wonder why he hadn't agreed to purchase Jess's staid choice, which would at least have given him chance to relax.

As if by some silent signal the excited chatter surrounding him died down. There was a rustle of best clothes as everyone stood up. A few more tense seconds passed and then a guitar began to strum, announcing the arrival of the bride. A collective sigh went up, but Dante was facing forward. He was no romantic and was more concerned about Jess's absence. The seat he had saved for her was still empty. Was something wrong?

He focused his attention of Manuel, Maria's soon-to-be husband. The man appeared to be overwhelmed with emotion. He'd never seen Manuel cry. He might well cry with a lifetime of hen-pecking ahead of him, Dante reflected.

A waft of unbelievably agreeable perfume accompanied by the rustle of delicate fabric finally forced him to turn around. To say he was stunned by Maria's arrival would be seriously understating the case. But he was looking past Maria to her one and only bridesmaid, Señorita Jessica Slatehome.

This was Jess as he'd never seen her before. Dressed in a gown so ethereal and lovely it belonged in a painting rather than on a living, breathing woman—or it would have done, had that woman not been Jess. He was also struck by the fact that Jess had made no attempt to overshadow the bride. He'd seen that before, but Jess had chosen to wear very little make-up, and must have directed the hairdresser to draw her hair back demurely at the nape of her neck, rather than allow it to cascade down her back in all its fiery rippling glory. She wore no jewellery to catch the eye, though it occurred to him she might have none to wear...

Sensing his interest, she turned her head to look at him. Her face was perfectly composed, though her em-

erald eyes held enough of Skylar to make him antici-
pate the rest of the day even more than he had expected.

And then she was gone.

Moving on down the aisle until she came to a halt
behind the bride and groom, Jess shattered his honour-
able resolutions and left Dante counting the seconds
until he could be with her again.

Jess hadn't been to many weddings, and though she had
a few ideas about the high-octane atmosphere on such
occasions she could never have anticipated the level of
testosterone at this one. Dante's wranglers were young,
tough and high-spirited, while Maria's relatives were
gitanos, experts in the art of flamenco with their own
customs and language.

Maria's people had enriched Spanish culture for
centuries with their valuable contribution of music and
dance and finely crafted wares, and many of the young
women who had travelled down from their mountain
villages were extremely beautiful. Safe to say, Dante's
ranch hands were on full alert.

Dante had instructed his people to erect the marquee on the paddock closest to his ranch house. The
path leading up to it was lined with candles and flowers while the inside of the tent was a riot of music, excited guests, colourful clothes and flashing jewellery.
Blooms so perfect they hardly looked real filled the
air with exotic scent, but what touched Jess the most
was the sight of the toughest men with their recently
smoothed-down hair and newly shaven faces. All except for Dante, who had gone for his customary rug-

ged look, and who, apart from his dark, custom-made suit, managed to look as swarthy and as dangerous as he ever had.

Concentrating fiercely on Maria so as not to be distracted by him, Jess found tears pricking the back of her eyes. Maria had never looked more beautiful in a wedding gown that gave more than a passing nod to the flamenco tradition of her kin. It would be no exaggeration to say that Maria had been transformed from diligent housekeeper to fairy tale bride.

Who didn't love a wedding? She couldn't help but glance at Dante, and there was her answer. Maria had already told her he'd refused a seat of honour at the front, as Dante believed that was where Maria's relatives should be seated. In a position halfway down the aisle, he was already restless. Dragging her attention away, she was just in time to take Maria's bridal bouquet as the ceremony began.

Incense swirled while soft words of praise were spoken, though through it all an underlying tension and discreet glances suggested the congregation's thoughts were already turning to more earthly pleasures.

When the ceremony ended Maria called out excitedly, 'I'm married! I'm married!'

To which her new husband replied in a rather different tone, '*Terminado! Ya he terminado!* I'm done for! I'm done for!' which set the entire place rolling with laughter.

'You may kiss the bride…'

The poor priest battled in vain to restore order to a congregation that was more interested in partying.

Everyone was on their feet, cheering and applauding, while Maria, being tiny, disappeared completely behind a wall of guests. The first intimation Jess received that the bride was safe was when the bridal bouquet came sailing over the human barricade to land squarely in the centre of her chest. Cradling it close to keep it from being trampled, she backed straight into a roadblock that turned out to be Dante Acosta.

'I'm getting you out of here before you're squashed to a pulp,' he informed her.

'You're not using your stick.'

'Thanks for reminding me,' Dante growled as he forged a passage for them through the crowd. The throng parted like the Red Sea to allow him through, and it was only when he had her safe on the fringes that Dante relaxed and turned to face her. 'You sure you're okay?'

'Thanks to you, even Maria's bouquet made it through.'

'You know what this means, don't you?' Dante prompted as he stared at the lush arrangement Jess was holding close to her heart.

'Maria can dry the flowers and keep them?' Jess suggested, tongue in cheek.

Dante huffed at this. 'Trust you to strip the romance out of it.'

'Me?' Jess queried. 'Like you're so romantic?'

'I do have my moments, given half a chance.'

Excitement and jealousy roiled inside her. It was a flippant remark. Dante made it while they were eye-balling each other, but it was enough to rouse Jess. Neither emotion was appropriate, so she quickly moved on to professional concerns. 'Where's your cane?'

'Thanks to you, I don't need it so much.'

'You'll need it tonight. You'll be on your feet a lot.'

Dante speared her with a look. 'Okay, *señorita*, so I left it by the table. Is that good enough for you?'

'You're learning,' she approved, holding his fierce look steadily.

'I've got the best of teachers,' Dante conceded with a look that sizzled its way through her veins, leaving her breathless.

Approachable Dante was far more dangerous than grim Dante, Jess concluded. His smile and the way he dipped his head to whisper in her ear made all her good intentions turn bad.

'Aren't the decorations lovely?' she blurted in a lame attempt to distract them both from the sexual tension between them. The boisterous congregation had spilled out of the seating area in front of the altar, which meant the quiet place Dante had found for them would soon be swamped.

'These pine cones remind me of home at Christmas,' she admitted wistfully as they moved on to the shade of an awning decorated with swags and bows.

'Maria's people brought them from the mountains where they live. It was Maria's dream to have everything reflect her heritage today.'

'Which you've helped her achieve, and beautifully.'

'She's worth it. I'd trust Maria with my life.'

'What will you do for Christmas?' Maria had explained she was taking time off for a honeymoon, so there would be no one else living in the house, as far as she knew. 'Will you join family?'

'Why are you so interested?'

Jess shrugged. 'I'm not. I just don't like to think of people being alone at such a special time of year. I'd never leave my father at Christmas, but don't worry, your treatment can safely be handed over by then,' she hurried to reassure Dante. 'And if you stick to your regime you could be back on the polo field by New Year.'

Breath shot from her lungs as Dante lifted her up in his arms. Until she realised he was moving her out of the way of the wait staff.

'Don't squash the flowers!' she exclaimed to cover her breathless shock and excitement.

'I'll have them delivered to Maria,' Dante offered. 'Or do you want to hang on to them for some reason?'

'What reason?' Jess demanded. 'Do you think I'm going to take a turn around the marquee to try and drum up some interest?'

'Now I'm offended,' Dante protested, hand on heart.

She thought of the snarling wolf beneath. 'You?' she queried. 'The only certainty about you is that you enjoy teasing me. Would you care to accompany me so you can make a list of my potential suitors?'

He stared at her darkly for a moment, then laughed. They both laughed, and both relaxed. 'I think the bride's calling you,' Dante prompted. 'You'd better go and attend to your duties. How lucky am I,' he added as Jess turned to leave, 'to be spared the ordeal of trying to find you a mate?'

'A mate?' Jess queried, stopping to throw him a paint-stripping look. 'You should be so lucky.'

Dante's lips pressed down but his eyes were firing with laughter. 'When I lifted you, that was what your body told me you needed.'

'You and my body don't speak the same language,' she assured him in a flash. 'And now, if you'll excuse me—'

'And if I don't?'

She stared at Dante's hand on her arm.

'It would be my pleasure to escort you to Maria's table,' he murmured.

'There's no need. I can find my way.'

'As I'm sitting next to you and it's my table too, it would seem sensible for us to walk there together.'

There was nothing sensible about this, Jess reasoned as she paused. 'It seems I have no option,' she said at last.

'None at all,' Dante agreed.

Conversation between them and the other guests was lively at the top table, but on one of their many tours around the marquee to make sure everyone had everything they needed it was inevitable that Jess encountered Dante. What she hadn't expected was that he would catch her around the waist and whirl her on to the dance floor. 'You can enjoy yourself too,' he insisted when Jess protested that she had her duties to attend to.

'Your duty is to check on me and make sure I don't overdo it,' he informed her.

'And how am I supposed to do that when you never listen to a word I say?'

'My recovery would argue otherwise. You can gauge the extent of my recovery as we dance.'

And a number of other things, she thought hotly as Dante drew her close. 'I'm not sure it's appropriate.'

'Uncertainty doesn't become you, Señorita Slate-home. Should I doubt your prowess now?'

'Not where my therapy's concerned.'

'What else should I doubt?'

Jess's cheeks burned.

'If you don't want to dance with me, that's another matter,' Dante told her with a relaxed shrug of his powerful shoulders, 'but this is our promised dance—to celebrate my recovery,' he reminded her.

'I don't remember promising that.'

'Amnesia can be a terrible thing.'

'Don't make jokes. I know you're teasing me again.'

'Am I?'

Dante's voice was so warm and coaxing, and his body so hot and strong, that just for a moment she allowed herself to relax.

Of course she should have known better.

'I won't allow you to play the professional card at a wedding,' Dante warned, 'or assume the role of Cinderella. You can't run out on me at midnight.'

'So you're Prince Charming now?'

'I have a white horse.'

'And an answer for everything.'

'I do my best,' Dante agreed.

'If I agree to dance, it's only on the condition that you sit down and rest afterwards.'

'Rest?' Dante's lips tugged up at one corner in a smile. 'Not a chance,' he murmured dangerously close to her ear. 'A resting wolf is still a dangerous animal. Your treatment worked, and now you must take the consequences.'

Why did she choose that moment to stare up into Dante's laughing eyes?

'That's better,' he whispered, drawing her attention to his mouth. 'Relax. You have permission to enjoy yourself without feeling guilty.'

She drew in a shaking breath while Dante continued in the same soothing tone, 'You look beautiful tonight and, as Maria is happily entwined around her new husband, you're free of your duties, and free to dance with me.'

Oh, but this was dangerous. And irresistible. Wearing such a fabulous gown made Jess feel different, as if anything might be possible for the woman who wore the gown. When morning came she'd be a farmer's daughter again and see things differently, but for now...

Something fundamental had changed between them, Dante reflected as Jess quite clearly debated whether or not to move into his arms. She knew what that entailed as much as he did. It was line crossed that could never be redrawn. The tension between them was too much for that to happen. They knew each other better, and yet in some ways not at all. There were still too many pieces of the jigsaw missing. He had pledged to keep everything professional, and so had Jess. He wasn't satisfied with that. Was she?

What did she think about while he lay on the treatment couch beneath her hands? He had to try very hard not to think. Thinking was dangerous because the sight of her was enough to arouse him. Even the pain he suffered beneath her probing fingers aroused him. Everything about Jess was arousing, but the stakes were high because slaking his lust would never be enough where Jess was concerned. She was a special woman who demanded more of him emotionally than he had ever been prepared to give.

Banked-up feelings exploded inside her as Dante drew her into his arms. There was something so compelling and right about it, and that in itself made her wary. This wasn't just a dance; it was a barrier crashing down. It was permission to feel, to respond, to hope for something more. She'd been so careful around him up to now, not just because of professionalism. Natural caution played its part. Dante was a player in every sense of the word. His relationships were famously many and short-lived, though at the moment he was making her feel as if she was the only woman capable of reaching him. How many others had he made feel that way?

He knew how to tease. Dante's grip was frustratingly light and stirred a primal need inside her. *Leave it at dancing or regret it in the morning*, were inner words of caution she ignored. Dancing like this was a prelude to sex. Every inch of her body was moulded to his. Dante was exerting no pressure, but Jess's body had its own ideas. His thigh was threaded through hers, bringing them into the closest contact possible outside of sex. But how—*how*—was she supposed to resist him? And did she want to?

'You seem distracted,' Dante commented when the first dance ended.

'Nothing could be further from the truth,' she assured him. 'I'm wide awake.'

'And firing on all cylinders,' he observed, bringing her with him as the band started playing again.

She should have stopped at that point, excused herself politely and left the floor. Instead, she warned, 'Behave yourself or I'll make you sit down to rest that leg.'

'I love that you're so masterful,' Dante mocked in a husky whisper, bringing his mouth very close to hers.

'And I love that you accept my authority,' Jess countered with a half teasing smile. She couldn't be serious all the time. 'At one point I thought I'd have trouble with you.'

'You will,' Dante promised, drawing her closer still.

Dancing with Jess was like seizing hold of a red-hot brand and asking to be consumed by it. Any lingering thought he might have had that they could rewind to achieve their previously careful and polite relationship was now implausible, impossible; it just couldn't happen. It only took millimetres of subtle shift in their bodies to tell him Jess felt the same. There was no need for grandiose gestures or unnecessary words between them. Coming together like this was enough. No woman had ever felt so right in his arms or been so receptive. There were a lot of beautiful women at the wedding but there was only one Jess. Who made him laugh as she did? Who had the wit to exchange banter that could be funny but was never cruel?

'This is better than I thought,' she whispered, surprising him with her boldness, and yet not really surprising him at all.

'Better still,' she murmured when he drew her close.

Jess's duties as bridesmaid were the only obstacles he faced. She had a keen eye for detail and noticed everything, which meant leaving his side on a number of occasions to help the wait staff or to answer a guest's query. Nothing was too much trouble for Jess. Apart from dancing with him, apparently. By now they should be somewhere else, but he hadn't bargained on dancing with a Girl Scout.

God bless the Scouts, he reflected, shaking his head with amusement as Jess embarked on yet another mission. He might as well go rest his leg.

The party went on late into the night. When Maria teased Jess into joining her in dancing on the table, Jess laughed. 'I hope you know I've got two left feet.'

'Too late now,' Maria told her as the bridegroom, Manuel, lifted Jess and deposited her next to his bride. Guests had gathered to watch the spectacle, which meant Jess couldn't let her new friend down.

'Lift your gown like this,' Maria instructed as she picked up the hem of her wedding dress to strut a few dramatic flamenco steps. 'Arch your back and stamp your feet in time to the music. Clap your hands like this.'

Having been forced to borrow shoes that were be-coming increasingly uncomfortable, Jess confined herself to a series of poses and enthusiastic shouts of *'Olé!'* Carried away by the excellence of Maria's danc-ing, she acted on a wave of enthusiasm, so when the music ended and Maria jumped into her bridegroom's arms, Jess jumped too—straight into the arms of Dante Acosta, who'd been standing watching with a look she found impossible to interpret. Catching her with no effort at all, he carried her away through the crowd.

So much for her resolve to keep Dante at arm's length, Jess mused, excitement mounting. This was a night to remember, and whatever came next she was more than ready for it.

CHAPTER TWELVE

THE HUNGER TO be alone with Jess had been burning a hole through his head throughout the entire wedding. He could think of nothing else but being alone with her, but once they were inside the ranch house he reined in the wolf. Lowering Jess to her feet, he stood in the shadows staring down. 'Another drink?'

'I haven't had a drink yet. Bridesmaid duties,' she reminded him. 'Clear head and all that?'

'Keeping a clear head is always wise.'

'With you around,' she agreed cheekily.

Angling her chin to stare up at him with that same playful, challenging look in her eyes, she plumbed some deep, untapped well inside him. This couldn't end here. It wouldn't end here. They continued to stare at each other until the tension snapped, he seized her hand and they headed for the stairs—ran, rushed, with no sign of his injury now. Jess was the woman who'd broken through his reserve, and they were both laughing. It felt good after so long of having nothing to laugh about. Humour was a healing balm, and it was a glorious irony to want Jess so badly and yet be laughing so much that they couldn't get there fast enough. Tears of laughter were streaming down Jess's face as she finally dropped down on the stairs. He joined her and when eventually she fell silent that silence was charged with sexual energy. Who needed a bed?

'May I?' she asked, her voice hoarse with laughter.

'Do I have a choice, *señorita*?' he asked as she reached for his belt.

'None at all.'

Those were the last few moments of calm. The next saw them tearing at each other's clothes. Several of the tiny buttons down the back of the bridesmaid's dress bounced down the stairs and skittered across the floor in the hallway.

To hell with this! He had no intention of making love to Jess on a staircase.

'Dante! Give your leg a break,' she protested as he swung her into his arms.

'Why? If I injure it again, you'll have to stay on.'

'Dante, I can't do that. You know I can't—'

That was the last sensible conversation they had. It was as if an atomic force had consumed them both. Crashing into his room, he rocked back against the door, slamming it behind them. Lowering Jess to her feet, he wrenched off his jacket and tossed it on a chair as Jess slipped off her dress with catlike grace. Tugging his shirt free, Jess started work on his zip. At the same time they were kissing wildly, lips, teeth clashing in a dance as old as time. Animal sounds of need escaped their throats until finally he cupped Jess's face in his hands and silenced her with kisses that were deep and long.

'You're overdressed,' she complained when they came up for air.

'So are you,' he growled as he viewed her flimsy thong.

Cocking her head to one side, Jess smiled a witchy smile. 'Do you like it?'

His groin tightened to the point of pain. 'Depends on how easily it rips.'

'Why don't you try it and see?' she suggested.

It ripped.

When Dante touched her she was his—right away, no hesitation. Fears and consequences were instantly banished to a place so deep in her mind she doubted they'd ever break free. This was right. This was how it should be. Falling back on the bed, she pulled him down on top of her. Guiding his hand, she directed him shamelessly. Not that Dante needed much direction. Moving her hand away, he continued to pleasure her in more ways than she knew existed.

'Don't,' she begged when he pulled away. She needed this—needed Dante. The world she had previously inhabited made no sense now. Without emotion, sensation or risk, it was empty, as everything else was without Dante.

'There are rules,' he informed her in a husky whisper.

'What? Like you make me wait? You leave me frustrated?'

'I make you show me what you want,' he added to her list.

'I can't do that.'

'Why not?' Dante enquired with his mouth very close to hers.

Jess's heart thumped wildly. Surely Dante couldn't mean she should touch herself in front of him?

'You're not shy,' he observed in a clinical tone, 'and we both know how hungry you are.'

'Just as I know you're teasing me.'

'Am I?'

Emotion churned wildly inside her. All her adult life she'd had disappointing sexual encounters, and these had left Jess with the firm belief that the pleasure everyone talked about must be overrated. So what did she want Dante to do about it? Prove her wrong? Prove her so wrong she'd be in a worse state than before—wanting him with no possibility of ever having him? She'd end up as chaste as a nun.

'I feel as if I've lost you,' he remarked, staring down. 'If you've changed your mind—'

'I haven't changed my mind.' This was what she wanted. At least she'd have something to think back on.

She shivered with pleasure as Dante ran one slightly roughened palm down the length of her back. 'You're beautiful. Why make such a deal out of denying your-self pleasure?'

She was wedded to her career? That was a flimsy excuse. She wouldn't be the first professional to cross the line, nor would she be the last.

Dante had spoiled her for all other men when she

was just seventeen. Being older made the risk greater. Making love with Dante would reopen that wound and leave her worse off than before. So she was a coward, Jess concluded, destined to live out her life without knowing if sexual pleasure was even possible.

'I get that you need time,' Dante murmured, but that didn't stop him continuing to waken her body until she doubted it would ever sleep again.

'Not too much time,' she admitted dryly.

'What are you doing?' he asked as she moved down the bed.

Putting off the moment? Pleasing Dante? Both of those things.

What she discovered slowed her right down.

Were all men this...built exactly to scale?

'You'd better stop,' he advised.

'I've no intention of stopping.' Brave words, but was this even possible when it took both her hands to encompass him?

Jess won and for the first time ever he was glad to be on the losing side. Tangling his fingers in Jess's hair, he urged her on. Beyond intuitive, she knew everything about pleasure. Exploring with her lips, her hands and dangerously thrilling passes of her tongue, she cupped him with exquisite sensitivity, and then she teased him with the lightest flicks of her tongue. The instant she took him firmly in both hands, moving them steadily up and down the length of his shaft, she brought him to the edge in seconds.

Sucking the tip brought his hips off the bed. The

master of control was finding it hard to hold on. Pleasure built until it refused to be contained and with a roar of relief he claimed his release. What he hadn't expected was that Jess would scramble off the bed.

'I shouldn't be here,' she blurted out.

'Why not?' Catching her close, he searched her eyes. 'Jess, what's wrong?'

'You know this is wrong. I know it's wrong—'

'I know nothing of the sort,' he assured her. But the mood had changed and couldn't be recovered.

Swinging off the bed, he crossed the room naked. Jess was right to call a halt. What could he offer her? Very soon he'd be back on top, with a fast-paced life that demanded selfish focus. Polo took him around the world, as did his business. Jess deserved a man who'd be there for her, someone kind and steady who would treasure her as she deserved. He was not that man, though the thought of some unknown goon pawing her made him sick. That didn't change the facts. He had no right to hold her back from the happiness she deserved.

Bringing a robe from the adjoining bathroom, he wrapped it around her shoulders. He couldn't bear seeing her looking so vulnerable. He'd secured a towel around his waist, for her sake rather than his.

'I'm sorry if I led you on,' she blurted as she moved about the room, gathering up her belongings.

'What are you talking about?'

'You must know,' she insisted, halting with clothes bundled in her arms to turn and stare at him.

'I'm afraid I don't. You didn't lead me anywhere I didn't want to go. I thought that applied to both of us.'

'I should go,' she declared, scouring the room to make sure she hadn't left anything behind.

'Go,' he invited, spreading his arms wide.

He frowned as he watched her leave. Jess was a sensualist, and beautiful, and he had thought her eager to be with him. What on earth was going on in her head? Yes, she was a professional woman with a successful career, but why was she denying herself a life?

Why couldn't she accept pleasure for pleasure's sake? Jess reasoned as she rushed to her room in the guest wing of the *estancia*. Wasn't that what other people did? Where was it written that every relationship must be everlasting? Why couldn't she accept a night of passion with Dante and leave it at that? Was she really bound by duty, or by fear that her teenage dreams could be dust by the morning? Would any man succeed in challenging her belief that she was better on her own, to sort out her life, care for her father, progress her career—

And still be lonely?

Well done, Jess. Everything and nothing has changed.

After a sleepless night she went to the stables to check on the horses. It was early and the yard was mostly silent. The *estancia* had that morning-after feeling that so often hung over a venue after a big event like a soothing web of remembered music and laughter. The door to the facility slid open on well-oiled hinges, and it didn't take long for Jess to satisfy herself that her father's ponies were still happy and contented. Dragging deep on the familiar scent of warm horse and clean hay, she went to take up her usual perch on a hay bale. Tucked away in the shadows of a stable had always been Jess's safe place of choice. It gave her chance to think, to plan, to reflect, and thankfully not regret too much this morning. Life could continue as it always had, a Dante-free zone with no more wild thoughts at a wedding or anywhere else.

With a sigh, she rested back. Going without sleep had left her exhausted. The sound was a cue for Dante's big old dog Bouncer to come and nuzzle her leg. As if he understood the turmoil inside her and was determined to soothe her troubled mind, he settled himself down beside her. Resting his head on her lap, Bouncer exhaled heavily, which made tears sting Jess's eyes at the thought of leaving the *estancia*, and all the many things she would miss. When she should be thrilled that Dante was cured...

'Stealing my dog now?'

Breath shot out of her lungs, with surprise at seeing him and the horrified response to the film reel playing behind her eyes of their aborted love scene last night. 'Dante? What are you doing here?'

'Checking on the animals, like you. I didn't expect to find you here. But then again...'

'What?'

'This is exactly where I should expect to find you.'

'You know me so well,' she teased, trying to keep things light.

'Hardly at all,' he argued. Staring down with concern, he added, 'Are you okay?'

'Of course,' she blustered, stroking Bouncer's ears furiously.

'Hey, leave some of that for me,' Dante insisted as he hunkered down beside her. 'You're spoiling him.'

'And so are you,' she remarked with a smile as Dante fed his old dog some treats. How did anyone manage to look so laid-back and gorgeous so early in the morning—after everything that had happened last night? She felt like a failure, like a ragbag in banged-up jeans and a faded top. It didn't help that Dante was wearing exactly the same sort of clothes, because they only made him seem more tantalisingly attractive and out of reach than ever.

'I'm glad I caught you,' he said in the most relaxed tone ever. 'I have to cancel my eight o'clock therapy session because of some pressing business.'

Her face was burning red with thoughts of last night, and it was a relief to have this shift of focus forced on her. 'No problem,' she blurted on a tight throat. 'We can change the time.' Gently moving Bouncer's head from her knee, she stood up. Dante stood too. 'Any time to suit you,' she offered.

'Hey, you've fulfilled your contract, remember?'

Dante was smiling down as warmly as ever, so why was ice flooding her veins?

'Have this one on me?' she offered awkwardly.

'I would never take advantage of you.'

'Even if I want you to?' So now she sounded desperate. The humiliation of last night put another thought in her mind: Dante was done with amateur hour.

'I've arranged your flight home,' he said as if confirming this.

Yes, she'd half expected it, but still she was stunned into silence. It was as if the floor was dropping away beneath her feet, and she was dropping away with it.

'Thank you. That's very kind of you. I appreciate it' She spoke all the expected words on autopilot. Her lips felt numb, and she had to remind herself that she had always intended to be home in time for Christmas. 'Time flies,' she murmured distractedly.

'When you're enjoying yourself?' Dante suggested wryly.

'I enjoy seeing you without a cane,' she said honestly.

'My PA will be able to tell you all the details. You'll be escorted every step of the way—taxi home, et cetera.'

'Thank you,' she said again as Dante pulled away from the wall. He was clearly in a hurry to leave. 'Don't let me keep you.'

Instead of leaving, he took hold of her hands. 'Jess, this isn't over. I really do have business to attend to.'

'You don't have to explain to me.'

'I think I do. I'm not punishing you or sending you away. Last night was a learning experience for both of us.'

When he learned how unsophisticated she truly was and she learned that Dante was way out of her league.

'It's time for you to get on with your life,' he continued gently. 'You can't be on call here for ever. I don't want to restrict you, but I don't want to lose what we've got either.'

What had they got? What had she allowed them to have? She'd gone into something without thinking it through. Dante wasn't a half-measures man and she had tried to short-change him. And now she could do no more than stand rigidly to attention, not trusting herself to say anything more than, 'Thank you again. It's very kind of you to see to the arrangements.'

'It's not kind,' Dante argued. 'It's in your contract. You'll leave tomorrow morning. The car will collect you prompt at six. That should still give you time to pack your things and say your goodbyes today.'

How could she have forgotten that this was Dante Acosta, a member of the famous Acosta family, tech billionaire and world class polo player? Having recovered full use of his leg, Dante was no longer dependent on anyone, and he was obviously keen to move on—especially from an ingénue who knew next to nothing about sex.

'I thought you'd want the first available flight back, so you can prepare for Christmas at home with your father.'

'That's right. That's so thoughtful of you.'

'Will you need an extra suitcase?'

For two outfits and some knick-knacks she'd bought on the market? 'That won't be necessary, but thank you again.'

'Flight time okay for you?' Dante prompted.

Jess could only hope she didn't look the mess she felt inside. 'Perfect,' she lied. 'The flight's perfect.' Even Bouncer was looking at her with concern. Trust a dog to sense trouble. You couldn't fool an animal. 'I'll be ready to leave at six.'

'Good. Please don't worry about my ongoing treatment. I've already hired someone else to carry on where you left off.'

'Good idea,' she confirmed mechanically. Dante hadn't wasted any time, but when did he ever?

'I won't be slacking,' he promised with a smile.

'I would never think that of you.' To her horror a tear stole down her cheek.

'It's a big, burly man, in case you were wondering,' Dante informed her with a grin.

Try as she might, she couldn't feel light-hearted. She had to get away before a complete meltdown happened and she betrayed her true feelings with huge racking sobs. 'Physios come in all shapes and sizes,' she agreed with a tight smile. 'And I'm sure that whoever you've chosen will be very good.'

'He'd better be,' Dante agreed with a crooked smile. 'You set the bar pretty high.'

But her contract had ended. *Deal with it.* 'I'll leave my notes, though doubtless your new therapist will have his own ideas.'

'Jess—'

'That's okay. I always intended to be back home for Christmas.'

Extricating herself gently from Bouncer, who had wound himself around her like a comfort blanket, she dipped down to give the big yellow dog one last hug.

Dante blocked her way as she stood up to go. 'Your father will be pleased to see you.'

'I'll be pleased to see him,' she said on a throat turned to ash.

'I'd fly you back myself,' Dante explained as he held the door for her when they left the stables, 'but I have this business deal, and then my first team practice the day after tomorrow and I want to get some training in before then.'

'That's wonderful news,' she said truthfully.

'I know what you're going to say—don't overdo it,' Dante supplied. 'I promise I won't. I owe my recovery to you, and I'll never underestimate what you've done for me.'

And you for me, Jess thought as the curve of Dante's lips twisted her heart until she wanted to cry out in pain. *You've taught me never to be naïve again*, she concluded with her usual sensible self back in charge.

'It's my job,' she said, pinning a smile to dry lips as she shrugged.

How much more of this could she take? She was breaking up inside and desperate to put space between them. The last thing she wanted was to break down in front of Dante. What good would it do, other than make her look even more pathetic than she felt?

She was halfway across the yard when Dante caught hold of her arm. 'Was this just another job for you, Jess?'

There was no chance to hide the tears in her eyes, nor did she even try. 'I'll miss you,' she blurted. To hell with pride! What did pride count for in the end? What did she stand to lose when there was nothing left to lose?

'I'll miss you too,' Dante admitted.

'Just take care of those ponies—and yourself,' she insisted. 'Take care of Moon for me in particular. She needs a lot of attention.' Unlike her human counterpart, thankfully, Jess thought as she firmed her jaw.

'How can you doubt it?' Dante queried.

'I don't,' she said honestly. When it came to his animals, Dante's love and desire to care for them was as acutely honed as her own. It was just human beings outside his family and staff he had a problem with.

'We won't forget you on the *estancia*, Skylar,' he said dryly, standing back.

An ugly swearword came to mind when Dante mentioned Skylar. Sadly, her mother had been wrong. There was no magic in the name. There was just Jess. Hurting like hell.

CHAPTER THIRTEEN

SHE WOULDN'T CRY, Jess determined as she stood at the kitchen sink on Christmas Eve in Yorkshire. This wasn't about her, or missing Dante so much it made her heart drum a lament in her chest. This was about the village where she lived, and about her father and the wonderful pals who had kept him afloat while she was working. This year, thanks to the sale of the ponies, they could afford a real Yorkshire Christmas, which meant she could thank everyone by holding open house as her mother used to do.

The scene beyond the steamed-up window would be perfect for a Christmas card. The snow fairies had arrived early this year, frosting the paddocks with pristine white, capping the fences with sparkling meringue peaks of snow. Her father had been out most of the day with the other local farmers, scouring the moors for stranded animals. They deserved a good feed when they got back.

No longer a lonely widower crushed by grief, Jim Slatehome was part of the village again, and part of the horse world too, just as her mother would have wanted. Of course he felt sad and still missed his wife, but now, thanks to all his friends and the medical help he had finally agreed to accept, he had strategies to deal with black moments, which was the most anyone could hope for.

Everything was right with the world, Jess told herself firmly as she put the finishing touches to the feast she'd prepared. Everything apart from one notable thing, she accepted with a pang. Where was Dante? What was he doing this Christmas? It made her unhappy to think of him alone. Surely he'd be with his family? It was such a big family.

Dante playing gooseberry? Did that seem likely?

If only he lived closer, she would have swallowed her pride and invited him over. *If only.* What an overworked phrase. It was no use to anyone, because it spoke of regret and things left undone.

So where was he?

According to her most reliable informant, the *Polo Times*, Dante Acosta had already whupped three types of hell out of his arch rival, Nero Caracas.

He'd better not have damaged that leg.

She'd researched the man who had taken over Dante's treatment and, to be fair, his reputation was impeccable. Trust Dante to choose the best.

It was the most frustrating thing on earth to care as deeply as she cared for Dante, Jess reflected as she pulled away from the sink, and yet be prevented from caring *for* him. He'd never played so well, according to *Polo Times*. And in a direct quote from Dante, that was all thanks to his physiotherapist, Jess Slatehome, who, together with her close associate Skylar Slates, had raised him up when he'd been down.

Dante had more than kept his promise to let the polo world know that Jess was good at her job. The phone had been ringing off the hook since the article was printed. Admittedly, most of the calls had been from reporters wanting to know what the 'real' Dante Acosta was like.

'He's such a loner and an enigma,' they'd prompted, 'while you were a young woman on her own.'

'I'm a medical professional with a job to do,' she had reminded them, remembering to add, 'Happy Christmas,' genuinely and warmly—because, like her, they were only doing their job.

Happy Christmas.

Jess's mouth twisted with the pain. She missed Dante so much the words meant nothing. Swiping tears away, she cleaned down the kitchen until it gleamed like never before. Checking the fire, she hung up her apron. With a shake of her head, as if that might knock some sense into it, she thought through the rest of the day. The food was ready. There was nothing more to do, and she longed to get outside. There could be more sheep to find.

He could go anywhere for Christmas. Invitations were stacked up in a pile on his desk at the *estancia*. Those from his family had received polite refusals. Those who craved Acosta glitter to brag about went in the bin.

He checked again. Nothing from Jess.

Why should there be?

Shifting position impatiently, he picked up a call from his sister, Sofia. 'Yes?'

'Compliments of the season to you too,' she said dryly. 'I gather you're in a good mood.'

'What do you want?'

Accustomed to his stormy moods since the injury, Sofia gave his bad manners a bye. 'I'm ringing to tell you not to buy so many presents. A truckload arrived today, when all we want is you.'

'Another year, perhaps,' he promised gruffly.

The Acostas always gathered at Christmas to remember their parents, though all five of them under one roof for any length of time could be a recipe for disaster. To put it mildly, they could be fiery. Dante's eldest brother always referred them to the Argentinian branch of the family which, he insisted, was far better balanced since all the brothers had married. He tried this same lecture each year but, as he remained unattached, it lacked bite.

The problem, Dante reflected, was that none of them was prepared to risk their heart after the crushing grief of losing their parents.

Even him?

Why couldn't he date Jess in a way she'd find acceptable? What was stopping him giving her the future she deserved?

Only his stubbornness. And possibly Jess's too.

Glancing at the phone, he felt a stab of regret. He loved his sister, and would miss catching up with Sofia and his brothers at the annual get-together, but this year there was only one place to be.

Why the change of heart?

Try living anything approaching a normal life with one exceptional woman, with whom he had unfinished business, permanently lodged in his mind.

Everything was ready for whoever dropped by, Jess reassured herself as she left the farm. Gifts for her father were wrapped and ready, together with the 'little somethings', as her mother used to call them, for his pals, and for any surprise visitors. She'd brought in extra folding chairs from the barn, so all that remained was to tempt her father back to the house with the promise of a delicious feast.

Financially, the year had ended on a high, mainly thanks to Dante's purchase of their ponies. It was a real treat to have enough money to buy her father things he'd denied himself for far too long. There would be a satisfyingly large heap of gifts beneath a tree laden with baubles that carried memories. Everything was warm and welcoming, just as her mother would have wanted it to be. The tradition of open house at Bell Farm would continue.

She paused at the top of a rise to stare out over the winter wonderland with its coating of snow and inevitably her thoughts turned to Dante.

Where was he? Who was he with? What was he doing? Would he be lonely? Was his leg still okay?

'Stop it,' she said out loud. This was going to be a wonderful Christmas, to which her broken heart was most definitely not invited.

* * *

Dante's flight through thunderclouds on his way from Spain to England was, to put it mildly, interesting, even in the luxurious surroundings of his private jet. The drive to the farm was even more so. No one was prepared to release a helicopter in such uncertain weather, so he hired a big workhorse-style SUV, but even that was brought to a sliding halt by snowdrifts on the exposed Yorkshire moors.

Grinding his jaw, he grabbed some belongings and set off to walk to the farm. According to the satnav on his phone, he was close to his destination. This wasn't the way he'd planned to arrive, but Jess wouldn't care less if he arrived in a helicopter or on foot. Unimpressed by shows of wealth, she was the most down-to-earth woman he'd ever met. She demanded an entirely new rulebook. He was still finessing the detail as he ploughed on through the snow.

He thought about Jess with each step, and what he owed her for restoring the strength in his leg. Most of all he thought about holding her. Maybe that was a stretch. There were no guarantees where Jess was concerned. She'd pick her own route through life.

Pausing to look around and get his bearings, he was grateful for the map on his phone. There were no recognisable landmarks. Everything was covered in a blanket of snow. Even the road had become one with the field. Jess's home turf seemed determined to show him an increasingly hostile face. If Jess did the same, he was wasting his time.

Pulling up his jacket collar, he pushed on. There

was an occasional flicker of light and a glimpse of colour down the hill, where a cluster of homesteads sat squat in the snow. He exhaled on a cloud of humourless laughter. Why was he surprised that a woman from such a bleak and forbidding landscape would be anything but strong and self-determining?

It had occurred to him that Jess might refuse to see him. Who rocked up unannounced on Christmas Eve? It couldn't be helped. He wasn't going anywhere until they met up face to face. Jess had rocked his world on its axis and there was no way he'd let this go. If he reached the village—*when* he reached the village, Dante amended—he'd surely find lodgings for the night. The roads were impassable, so he was stuck here whether Jess agreed to see him or not.

After another half a mile or so, he stopped to blink and rub snow from his eyes, seeing shadows moving in the distance. As he drew closer, he realised the shadows were men working in the field. Driven almost sideways by gusting wind, they were attempting to heave sheep out of a ditch. Several more animals were stranded, and he didn't hesitate before pitching in.

Fate had dealt him a kindness, Dante concluded as he worked with the other men. Rescuing the terrified animals built an instant camaraderie that allowed him to ask the way, enquire about lodgings and even learn something about Jess.

The moors had a peculiar stillness that only descended after a recent fall of snow. It was like being alone on the planet, without even birdsong to keep her company,

Jess mused as she trudged on. She was keeping a lookout for her father and for his friends, as well as any stranded animals she might find along the way. She'd come prepared, with a snow shovel strung across her shoulder on a strap.

She paused for a moment when she got to the brow of the hill. The view was immense. Now the snow flurries had died down she could see right across the moors to Derbyshire. But it was only a temporary respite because snow had started falling again.

Bringing her muffler over her mouth, she prepared to slither down what was now a treacherous slope. Halfway down, she dug in her heels and skidded to a halt. An SUV was stuck in a snowdrift and tilted on its side. Thoughts flashed through her head. Uppermost was saving whoever was in the vehicle before they froze to death. Hurtling down the bank regardless of safety, she sucked in great lungsful of air. She had to conquer that panic. She'd be no use to anyone like this.

Once she'd gathered herself, another question occurred: who drove a flashy SUV in the village?

Could it be Dante?

Don't be ridiculous, she railed at her inner voice. Why would Dante come here on Christmas Eve? There were no ponies to buy. He'd bought them all. And would a billionaire's Christmas include the simple pleasures of a small isolated village on top of the Yorkshire moors? He had absolutely no reason to come here.

That didn't stop her wading through the sometimes thigh-high snow. She had to reach the SUV. Not only would the driver and any passengers be in danger of freezing inside the vehicle; if they left it they could quickly become disorientated, and the result would be the same. Wind chill was deadly, and it was vital they reached safety and warmth soon.

Fast progress was impossible, which gave Jess's thoughts the chance to run free. Maybe Dante had somehow heard that Bell Farm was throwing its doors open to all-comers at Christmas. It wasn't beyond the bounds of reason that he'd spoken to her dad but, whoever was in that vehicle, or maybe wandering around lost on the moors, she had to do her best to find them.

There were times when Jess thought her feet would freeze into icicles and break off. This wasn't helped by the local brook being covered by a thin layer of ice beneath a concealing carpet of snow. She yelped as her feet sank beneath the surface yet again, but now she was within touching distance of the vehicle and she pressed on.

Swinging the snow shovel off her shoulder, she braced herself for whatever, or whoever, she might find inside. Was she too late? What if Dante had driven up to the moors? Why hadn't she had the courage to tell him how she felt before now? It wasn't as if she was shy or retiring. Tears froze on her face as she frantically dug out the snow. Why had she never told him she loved him? Why had she held back?

Why had they both held back?

It wasn't as if Dante had plied her with words of love and reassurance, any more than Jess had unleashed her true feelings for him.

Straightening up, she eased her aching back. It

wasn't as if they hadn't talked, but neither of them was comfortable talking about feelings. They'd both built grief-driven barricades. Was that what those they'd lost would want for them?

Please, please, please! Don't let it end like this, she begged the fates and anyone else who was listening. *Please let me have one last chance to tell Dante how I feel. I promise I won't shy away from it.*

There was no way of predicting, of course, how Dante might respond to that, but as he was hardly likely to be the driver of the vehicle that hardly mattered.

But there was no one in the SUV, and fresh snow had covered any footprints around it. Planting her shovel, Jess flopped down in the snow. Exhausted and dispirited she might be, but she couldn't spare the time to catch her breath. Getting up again, she resolved to solve the mystery of the abandoned SUV because whoever had been driving was still in danger.

She'd search the whole damn moor if she had to, Jess determined as she stumbled on. Thank goodness she knew the terrain.

CHAPTER FOURTEEN

'Jess?'

'Dante!'

Out of the blizzard came a shape: a man—the only man—a powerful, healthy, vigorous life force in a world grown so bleak and frightening even Jess had begun to doubt that it would ever be summer again.

She went rigid at first and then started laughing and crying at the same time, before launching herself at Dante. 'I can't believe you're here! I'm so glad you're safe!' Pulling back, she searched his eyes with relief.

'Believe,' he said dryly, gently disentangling himself.

'Were you in the SUV?' she demanded, swinging around to look over her shoulder.

'I had that pleasure.'

'Of landing in a ditch?' she suggested, laughing with happiness now.

'That was somewhat unexpected,' he conceded.

'So why are you here?' She was breathless with excitement.

'I keep asking myself that same question.'

Her eyes narrowed with suspicion. 'No one arrives on top of the Yorkshire moors in a blizzard without a very good reason. And it's Christmas Eve,' she pointed out, 'so it must have been something big to bring you here.'

Something small, he thought, measuring her fragility against the frozen landscape, but if you added spirit into the mix Jess was a match for any and all conditions.

'Are you saying I've got no excuse to be here?'

'Not unless you're hiding the reindeer.'

His lips tugged with the urge to laugh. Suddenly the trip was more than worthwhile. But there was something he had to know. 'Good surprise, or bad?'

'Lucky for you that you're in time to eat with us,' Jess exclaimed happily without attempting to answer his question.

'I wouldn't dream of putting you to that trouble.'

'No trouble,' she said, cocking her head to one side to bait him with a grin. 'We've got enough food for an army, so I could do with another mouth.'

'*Dios*, no!' he murmured dryly. 'I can't imagine you with another mouth. One is enough to contend with.'

She smiled and relaxed at this. 'But you will come and join us?' she pressed.

'I'd be delighted to join you. Solely in the interest of helping you out on the food front, of course.'

'Of course,' she teased back. 'Great!' Biting down on her bottom lip, Jess shook her head as she smiled up at him, as if she couldn't believe the evidence of her own eyes.

The force of Dante's personality alone was like a blaze of fire in a frozen monochrome landscape. Jess's feelings were in danger of overflowing. It was as if her world had exploded into a blizzard of happiness. Beyond relieved to have solved the mystery of the missing driver in the stranded SUV, she knew now that nothing could be better than discovering the driver was Dante.

'You're safe,' she marvelled as they walked along.

'That I am,' Dante confirmed while she imprinted every rugged detail of his face on her mind.

Of course he was safe. Dante Acosta would never set out on a mission without proper planning first. Hence the backpack and the storm-proof clothing and the tough workmanlike boots. The question was: what was his mission this time? Jess wondered.

Meeting up with her father and his friends a little way closer to the farm was such a happy reunion. 'So you found her!' Jess's father enthused, slapping Dante on the back as if he'd known him all his life.

'Have you two met already today?' Jess asked, cocking her head to one side to study both men.

'We met in the field where your father was rescuing sheep,' Dante revealed.

'And you joined in,' Jess guessed. Her father confirmed this with his customary grunt that reminded her so much of Dante.

Dipping his head, Dante whispered in her ear, 'We have to stop meeting like this.'

You have to stop sending shivers spinning down my

spine when my father is watching, Jess thought. 'Suits me,' she said coolly.

Meaningful glances exchanged between Dante and her father made Jess instantly suspicious. 'What's going on?' she prompted. 'What aren't you telling me?'

'This is no place to linger for a chat,' her father scolded gruffly.

There was nothing underhand about Jess's father. If he knew something he spat it out. This behaviour wasn't like him. She frowned. Her father wasn't frowning. A smile had spread across his face as he walked along with Dante. It was almost as if he had expected their visitor—if not today, then at some point soon. What weren't they sharing? Why had Dante come to Yorkshire?

'We'll take these sheep back to the barn,' her father was telling Dante. 'And then I hope you'll join us for our first Christmas feast.'

'I'd love to,' Dante confirmed.

'Excellent,' her father exclaimed, slapping his hands together to keep them warm. 'With Jess's cooking I can confidently guarantee you a very happy Christmas!'

'Happy Christmas to you too,' Dante echoed with an unreadable glance at Jess. 'And the best of everything in the New Year.'

'The New Year's going to be so much better for us,' her father enthused. 'You made sure of it,' he told Dante.

How had Dante made sure of it? The sale of the ponies would only take them so far. Jess didn't have chance to think it over as the group of men with her father chorused in a shout, 'Happy Christmas!'

Having seen the sheep safely gathered in, they ended up at the packed pub where, as Jess might have expected, her father invited everyone back to the farm. Steam rose from their clothes as the roaring log fire did its work. While the general air of celebration and good-humoured complaints about the weather rang out around her, Jess's focus was all on Dante. He bought a round of drinks for everyone and was soon swapping stories with the best. Not once did he let on that his life was extraordinary, and though the locals might have known he was a polo-playing billionaire, as far as they were concerned he'd helped them save the sheep, and that made him one of them.

It was wonderful to have Dante here in the place she loved best. And at Christmas, Jess's favourite time of year. Most important of all, he was safe. Why he'd come to the village didn't matter. All she cared about was that they were together. Dante was the best Christmas gift of all.

The farmhouse kitchen was almost as crowded as the pub and definitely as noisy, and in all the right ways. He was instantly struck by the warm and homely atmosphere Jess had created. She was special. This was special. With enough delicious food to feed an army and an assortment of chairs and stools gathered from who knew where, she soon had her visitors munching happily.

'I'm sorry,' she said as she squeezed past with yet another oven dish brimming with crunchy golden roast potatoes. 'This can't be what you're used to.'

She was gone before he had chance to tell her that this was so much better than anything he had, and that he envied everything about it. No Michelin starred restaurant could better the happy family atmosphere Jess had created here.

He'd never eaten food like it, and he prided himself on his chefs. If the way to a man's heart was through his stomach Jess had the route map down. They didn't have chance to speak as Jess was so busy, but he pounced on the cue when a rather attractive widow from a neighbouring farm invited her father over. 'I've got a room at the pub,' he told Jess, 'if you'd care to join me for a nightcap?'

'Why, Señor Acosta,' Jess challenged with a smile, turning her bright eyes up to his, 'are you propositioning me?'

'I'm offering to buy you a drink to thank you for the meal. Then I'll walk you home.'

And I'm supposed to believe it's as simple as that, her narrowed eyes clearly told him. Who could blame her when testosterone was firing off him in spears of hot light?

'Do you have people to look after the animals?' he asked.

'We drafted in some extra help over Christmas. They'll take it in turns to keep a watch through the night.'

'Then you have no excuse.' His lips pressed down as he shrugged.

'Apart from natural caution, do you mean?'

'What would Skylar say?' he challenged.

She laughed. 'I'm not sure I want to know.'

'You need a break so you can enjoy Christmas too,' he pointed out.

'You think?' Jess laughed as she wiped a forearm across her glowing face.

'I know it,' he stated firmly.

Her cheeks pinked up even more but she was in no hurry to give him her answer. *Brava*, Jess. This woman was exactly the challenge he wanted.

Should she go with Dante? Life was complicated, and he had made it even more so because she wanted to go with him, more than she'd ever wanted anything before.

There were so many reasons not to go. The kitchen was a mess—inevitable after a successful party—and she would have liked to stay and clear up.

'You go,' her father's friend Ella told her, having intuited Jess's dilemma. 'I'll handle this first thing tomorrow morning—and I'll handle your dad too.'

Jess could believe it as she exchanged a smile with the older woman. Ella coped with a farm on her own so there was no reason why she couldn't take on Jess's dad. 'If you're sure?'

'I'm positive. You've more than put the effort in to making today a great success, and if you can't go and have a quiet drink down the local pub I don't know what's wrong with the world.'

But would it be a quiet drink down the local pub? 'Thank you. You're very kind—'

Before Jess had chance to continue, her father interrupted with the surprising news that she shouldn't wait up for him.

'I don't know what time I'll be back,' he explained.

'Oh.' Jess's jaw must have dropped. She quickly pinned on a smile. Yes, she was surprised. Things seemed to be moving quickly between her father and Ella, though she'd been away in Spain and, with work and the animals, maybe it was Jess who was guilty for being out of the loop. She had never asked the relevant questions. Her father had been lost and lonely without her mother; why shouldn't he be happy now?

'See you, Dad,' she called out as he left with Ella. With all her heart, she wished them well, and her father a much better future.

They'd all come a long way, Jess reflected as the rest of their guests left for home. Dante was waiting by the door with her coat. So what was she going to do? Turn him down? She could stay here and nothing would change. He'd probably be gone by the morning. And what would she have missed?

That remained to be seen, she concluded, firming her jaw.

Glancing around the familiar kitchen, she couldn't help feeling that, whatever happened next, her life would never be the same again.

When he planned something, he planned down to the last detail. He'd taken the top floor of the pub in advance and had Christmas gifts for Jess and her father in his emergency backpack. He would arrange the recovery of the SUV as and when; meanwhile, champagne was on ice and, as he'd also requested, tasty snacks were in the icebox he'd had installed in one of the rooms. This wouldn't be his only visit to the village, so home comforts were essential. As for him and Jess? It was crucial they had a chance to talk in private.

Inviting her into the cosy sitting room, where the landlord had the good sense to light the log fire, he took her coat and then they stared at each other in silence.

Jess made the first move. Moving closer, she stood on tiptoe to brush her lips against his. 'That wasn't a mistake,' she informed him. With a shrug she added, 'Maybe it was as reckless as when I was seventeen, but I think I'm old enough to handle the consequences now.'

'You expect consequences?' He smiled and shook his head.

'You'd better not disappoint,' she warned cheekily.

'What's been holding you back?'

Jess's mouth twisted as she turned serious to think about this. 'Duty—like you? Career—like you?'

'Disappointments in the past?'

'If you think you can do better...'

She was only half joking, he suspected. 'Try me and find out.'

'I intend to.'

'Do you think you should take your boots off first?'

'My boots?' she echoed with surprise, glancing down.

'Your feet must be frozen.'

She stared at him and laughed. They both laughed, and were still laughing when he brought Jess into his arms to kiss her—gently at first, and then as if he would never let her go. Whatever doubts had been in Jess's mind, it soon became clear she'd given them the night off. Having left her boots by the door, she informed him, 'My heart is set on undressing you.'

He held his arms out. 'Be my guest.'

She did this slowly and deliberately, as if every button took her closer to a personal goal that had less to do with sex and more to do with establishing trust between them. His urges were far less worthy. He wanted to strip her naked, throw her on the bed and make love to Jess until she was too tired to move, but this was such a pivotal moment for both of them he decided to run with Jess's approach. Until she sank to her knees in front of him.

'Did I do something wrong?' she asked, wounded eyes fixed on his as he brought her to her feet.

'You've done nothing wrong,' he said gently. Now he understood why Jess's sex life had been so disappointing. If she'd had to do all the work, what pleasure was there in that for Jess? Sex should be a shared experience with mutual pleasure.

Swinging her into his arms, he carried her into the bedroom. 'Now it's my turn,' he warned as he peeled off the heavy socks she was wearing beneath her boots. 'These are disgusting.' He tossed them aside as she laughed, and then she took turns smiling and groaning with pleasure as he warmed her feet in his hands.

'You know all the best routes to a girl's heart.'

'Dealing with frozen feet is my speciality,' he conceded as he bathed her tiny feet in kisses and hot breath.

'How many hearts have you broken with that technique?'

'I've never been much interested in finding my way to anyone's heart,' he admitted.

She seemed surprised so he asked, 'Why do you find that so hard to believe?'

'Your reputation precedes you?' she suggested.

'Do you believe everything you read?' When she shrugged, he explained, 'I love my brothers and my sister, Sofia. And, before you ask—no, I have never put their feet near my mouth.'

Everything changed in that moment. Jess's smile broadened until it lit up her face, and he knew that the biggest hurdle had been crossed. Before sex came trust, and he had won Jess's trust.

CHAPTER FIFTEEN

DANTE UNDRESSED HER with as much care as he might have shown a skittish pony—if that pony had been wearing ten layers of Arctic gear. And with each item of clothing he removed, he kissed her. When she was naked the room seemed to grow very still. The only sound was their breathing—Dante's steady and Jess's interrupted by short gasps of pleasure when Dante found some new place to kiss.

It was possible to soothe and arouse at the same time, she was fast discovering, and Dante was a master of the art. Long, soothing strokes down her back quietened her, but made her want so much more. He gave her chance to feel her body waking to his touch, but his restraint was a torment. The urge to take the lead began to overwhelm her, but each time she tried to make a move Dante dissuaded her with kisses, telling her to concentrate on sensation and nothing else.

She hadn't just stepped over that line; she'd leapt over it, Jess concluded as a soft moan of pleasure escaped her throat. They could never be close enough and when Dante's hand found her she cried out loud with excitement. He'd made her wait so long she was right on the edge. 'Please don't stop,' she begged when he moved his hand. His answer was to kiss her neck, her lips, her cheeks and her eyes, while she trembled with anticipation beneath him like a greyhound in the traps. Then he turned her and, holding her hands in one giant fist above her head, he made control impossible. As she bucked uncontrollably beneath him Dante released her pinned hands and captured her thrusting buttocks in one hand while he helped her to extract every last pulse of pleasure with his other hand. Having found her slick warmth, he made her take the short journey again, until she found herself right on the edge.

'Again?' he suggested in a low growl.

She had no chance to do anything but cry out, 'Yes!' Dante's fingers were magic and he knew just what to do. Grinding her body frantically against the heel of his hand, she claimed her second powerful release. He silenced her panting and groaning with a kiss that was as deep as it was tender.

She loved the way he held her buttocks firmly in place with one hand as he pleasured her with the other. 'Are you going to be as greedy as this all night?' he teased in a deep, husky tone as he loomed over her, swarthy and dangerous, and so impossibly sexy.

'You made me insatiable,' she said, marvelling at how gentle he could be, how persuasive. She was half his size and Dante treated her as if she were made of rice paper, which was frustrating but also reassuring.

'I want to taste you,' he growled, moving down the bed.

She laughed softly. 'Do I have a say in this?'

'No.' Lifting her legs onto his shoulders, Dante dipped his head.

She thought she knew pleasure? She was wrong. *This* was pleasure. This was something beyond anything else.

'I can't,' she protested, speaking her thoughts out loud. 'Not again.'

'Is that a fact?' Dante queried with a wicked look, pausing.

His tongue, his mouth and fingers continued to work their magic. This time the pleasure waves were so strong she was tossed about on a wild tide of sensation that stole away every thought except one: could she remain suspended in Dante's erotic net for ever?

Jess...

Holding himself back was the biggest test he'd ever faced. Jess took even longer to recover and when she did her eyes were heavy. She wasn't just tired; she was exhausted. It had been a long day, with the shock of seeing him and the rescue of the sheep. Then she'd gone on to cater a meal for who knew how many before allowing herself downtime. Who wouldn't be exhausted? Taking her now would be taking advantage. She was sleepily sexy but her conscious mind was taking a well-earned breath. He'd waited a long time to make love to Jess and when it happened he aimed for special, not something to tag to a long, draining day.

'You're smiling,' she commented drowsily.

Because he wasn't used to waiting, but Jess was different.

'Well?' she prompted softly, reaching out. 'Are you going to explain?'

Turning off the light, he drew her into his arms.

'Are you asleep?' she asked when some quiet time had passed. 'Do you regret this?'

'No.'

'Then…?'

'You're tired,' he murmured.

'I'm not,' Jess protested.

'Exhausted, then.'

'I do need a hug,' she admitted.

To reassure her, he tightened his grip.

'I don't want you to think I'm having second thoughts,' she whispered.

It was obvious she wanted to talk. Releasing her, he sat up beside her. 'Talk to me,' he encouraged her gently.

'About loss and grief and duty, and how there's never enough time to mull over those things?'

'There hasn't been a right time for either of us, I'm guessing,' he admitted, raking his hair.

'Stop distracting me,' she scolded, smiling, 'or we're wasting another chance to talk it out.'

'I'm not even sure we should be talking about it now, when you so clearly need to sleep.'

Searching his eyes, she explained, 'I need to talk first and then sleep.'

'Go ahead,' he said softly, waiting.

'I didn't cry when my mother died,' Jess eventually

revealed in a small voice, as if she still felt guilty about it. But then, remembering his loss, she reverted to her customary warm, concerned self. 'I don't expect you showed any emotion either when you lost your parents.'

'Oh, I was angry,' he confessed, thinking back. 'When I arrived at the hospital one of the doctors told me, "Where there's life there's hope."'

'And of course you desperately hoped he was right and believed him.' Her eyes were in that moment as she stared into his.

'There was no hope,' he confirmed flatly. 'My parents were already dead, as I discovered when I barged into the room where they had been treated.'

'You were how old?'

'Old enough to know better—seventeen or eighteen. I've found it hard to trust anyone outside my inner circle since that day.'

'And who could blame you?'

'Not you, apparently,' he remarked as he stared into Jess's eyes. 'So, what's your excuse for being so bottled-up?'

'Events,' she said succinctly in the way people did when there was a world of trouble hidden behind a single word.

'Tell me about those events,' he said gently. 'The grief you hid I know about, so I'm guessing we're talking about your father.'

She was silent for a while and then confessed, 'He was such a proud man...'

'Was?' he prompted.

'You must remember...' Her eyes were big and wounded.

'I do. Everyone's brought low by grief, so I'm guessing your father took some time to pull through.'

'It wasn't easy for him.'

'Or for you,' he observed quietly.

'Don't they say love makes anything possible?'

She looked so sad as she asked the question. His imagination could fill in the blanks for now. Jess wasn't ready to tell him the detail. Maybe she never would be. She was right about her father being a proud man, and Jess was as protective of family as he was. It was up to her to decide if and when and how much she told him.

'I trust you,' she admitted before falling into a thoughtful silence. 'I know you won't say anything to harm my father's reputation,' she added at last, staring into his eyes, unblinking.

'Never,' he pledged.

He let the silence hang until Jess was ready to continue. 'I built my adult life on the promises I made to my mother, which were to continue my education and to qualify so I could earn a living and look after my father and the farm. That didn't leave much time to mourn my mother's loss, but it was a relief to be busy because the alternative was to sink into grief and achieve nothing, which would have betrayed her trust.'

'We all need time to mourn.'

'Says you,' she rebuked him with a sad smile.

'Let's build on the past and remember those we loved happily, positively, knowing that's what they'd want us to do.'

'You always find a way to make me smile,' she observed thoughtfully.

'Do you want to punish me for that?'

'Do you want to be punished?'

His smile darkened. 'Not for that.'

Her gaze flew to the rumpled bed. 'You spoiled me for other men ten years ago.'

'That kiss in your father's stable?'

'That was just the start,' she admitted. 'And now you've spoiled me all over again.'

'Don't expect me to apologise.'

When he fell silent she asked, 'Dante, is something wrong?'

This was not the right time to explain what was happening with the farm. 'No. There's nothing wrong. We'll talk again in the morning.'

'Promise?' she asked softly.

'I promise.' Drawing Jess into his arms, he settled down on the bed. Feeling her tears wet his chest, he turned to look at her. 'Why are you crying?'

'I'm happy,' she confessed.

Cradling her in his arms, he kissed the top of her head. 'Sleep now. I'm not going anywhere.' She was possibly already asleep, he thought as Jess's breathing steadied, and he was surprised by the deep sense of satisfaction that stole over him at the thought that she could relax in his arms.

Was this love?

Deep trust was love. Unpacking memories that had wounded them both and entrusting them to each other was closer to love than anything else he could think of.

The warm contentment inside him felt like love. How else could he be lying here, wanting this woman as he did, without the slightest intention of disturbing her?

Had there ever been a better way to start Christmas Day than this? Jess woke slowly to find she was naked in bed with Dante in the dark quiet hours of early morning. Naked and contented, she amended, though not for long. It was a small step from lazy contentment to making her wishes clear, and Dante was as eager as she was. With a soft growl of cooperation, he shifted position to make things easier for her.

Guiding him, she used Dante's body to rouse a place that could never get enough of him, and now badly needed more.

'Hey,' Dante whispered, 'take it easy.' Moving over her, he whispered, 'There's no hurry.'

She was way past listening to advice, but when he allowed her the smooth tip of his erection she was more than ready to bow to his greater knowledge, especially as he had moved her hands by this time and taken over.

'When I say and not before,' he instructed.

How could she answer when all her concentration was focused on getting him to probe a little deeper? Dante's jaw was set, she noticed, glancing up. He was suffering too. So much restraint had to be torture for him. Damping down the urge to thrust forward and bring their torture to an end, she settled for doing as he suggested, which was to let everything go and allow Dante to set the pace.

'That's right… Relax,' he encouraged. 'Sensation

will be so much greater if you allow me to pleasure you, while you do absolutely nothing.'

Heaving a shaking sigh, she knew at once he was right. Each touch was amplified by her stillness. She could concentrate on every feeling as Dante pleasured her at his own pace. She tensed momentarily as he sank a little deeper, stretching her beyond belief. They weren't even past the smooth, domed head of his erection yet but, feeling her concern, he stopped to allow her to become used to the new sensation. When she was ready to move on, he cupped her buttocks and took her a little deeper still. There was no pain. He'd prepared her too well. There was only pleasure—wave after wave of incredible pleasure, fired by the overwhelming need to be one with him.

Sinking deeper still, he took her to the hilt in one slow, firm thrust. She couldn't help but gasp, but Dante had an answer for the shock of his invasion. Massaging her with rotating movements of his hips, he brought her swiftly to the point of no return and then he commanded in a low voice, 'Now.'

She didn't need any encouragement and plunged into pleasure with repeated cries of relief. Even when the waves crashing down on her eased off, Dante was still moving. He took her steadily and gently until her hunger built again, when she grasped his buttocks to work him faster and harder, and he pounded into her as if they would never ever stop.

Now the dam had burst their lovemaking was fierce. They enjoyed each other in as many ways as they could, gorging on pleasure, sometimes on the bed and sometimes not. A shared shower to cool down after more heated activity proved another excuse for lovemaking, only this time she scrambled up him and Dante slammed her against the wall to take her deep. Towelling dry was another opportunity to test the resilience of the black marble countertop, and when they returned to bed they didn't quite make it.

'Not so fast,' he said, dragging her close. Bending her over where she was standing at the side of the bed, he encouraged her to brace her hands against the mattress so he could take her from behind, while using his hand to encourage somewhere that needed no encouragement. He allowed her cries of release to subside before turning her so she was sitting on the edge of the bed, facing him. Moving between her legs, he pressed her back. Grabbing a pillow, he placed it beneath her buttocks.

There was no end to pleasure with your soulmate, Jess reflected some considerable time later when she sank back, gasping, on the bed.

What else could she call Dante? Could fate be so cruel that it had thrown them together again for no reason? The gulf between them remained wide in terms of financial success and lifestyle, but were these the most important measures? Wasn't the way they played off each other, and improved each other, far more important than that? Would this feeling of euphoria last? she wondered as she stared at Dante. Why not, she reasoned, when his care of her, and his sheer damn sexy self, was so different to the grim face he showed the world? Was that a coincidence too? Couples could destroy each other, while others were improved in every way just by being together. She wanted to believe that she and Dante were builders not destroyers, and that they would be stronger together than they were apart.

'It's your turn now?' she teased as Dante joined her on the bed.

She reached for him. They reached for each other. Dante took them both to the edge, and over it.

They slept for what must have been hours. When she woke the light was filtering through the curtains. Could it really be Christmas morning? Tiptoeing across the room, she tweaked back the edge of the curtain.

'Hey,' Dante complained huskily as light poured into the room. 'Don't you ever need to rest?'

Bouncing back on to the bed, she threw her head back with sheer happiness. 'Says the man who keeps more plates spinning than anyone I know?

'Happy Christmas! The best Christmas ever!' Tossing her hair back, she laughed with sheer happiness at the dawning of this special new day.

'Ah,' Dante said, sitting up. 'Thanks for reminding me—'

'You needed reminding? You are a lost cause.'

'Not quite,' he assured her. 'Let me grab a robe.'

'Wow. This sounds serious,' she said as Dante rolled out of bed. Her spirits took a dive when he didn't answer. 'While you do that, I'm going to take a quick shower.'

Freshen up, think, organise her brain cells. Last

night had been spectacular, but now it was another day. And she was determined to remain optimistic.

One of the advantages of Dante taking the entire top floor of the pub was that they didn't have to share a bathroom, so she luxuriated for quite a while before dressing and returning to the bedroom to find Dante seated at the desk. He'd showered too, and was dressed in jeans and a form-fitting top—a pairing that pointed up his spectacular physique. She didn't have long to dwell on that. There were some documents on the desk that somehow made her nerves twang. And Dante was looking serious. This wasn't good.

'Why are you frowning?' he asked.

'Am I?'

He gave her one of his amused, forbearing looks. 'I'm not allowed to give you a Christmas present?' he queried.

'Depends what it is. And I feel terrible,' she added.

'Oh?'

'I don't have anything for you,' she explained.

'But I'm not expecting anything,' Dante told her with a shrug. 'You didn't know I was coming.'

'I could have sent a card.'

'Write one now,' he suggested with a casual jerk of his chin in the direction of the pub's info pack, which would almost certainly contain some of the striking postcards they sold at the bar.

'I wouldn't know what to say,' she admitted honestly.

'Really?' Dante barked a short laugh. 'You being short of words must be a first.'

She hummed while her heart raced. What was Dante hiding in that case?

'Well?' he prompted as she hovered by the door. 'Are you coming in properly, or are you going out again?'

She shut the door, but stayed where she was.

'Don't you want to know what your gift is?' he coaxed.

'A halter and a bag of pony nuts?' she ventured, unable to rip her gaze from the official-looking papers.

Dante pulled a mock-disappointed look. 'Is that your best guess?'

'It's my only guess.'

'How would you feel if I said that this document is my way of gifting you the farm?'

As Dante held out an official-looking envelope time stood still. Jess didn't speak or move a muscle, and was completely incapable of rational thought.

'Well?' he prompted.

She attempted to moisten her lips so she could reply, but her mouth had turned as dry as dust. 'I'd say you were teasing me,' she said at last. 'But it isn't a very funny joke.'

'I'm not joking, Jess,' Dante assured her with a long steady look. 'That's why I've come here. Well, partly, anyway. I guess I could have sent the contract, but I wanted to hand it to you in person.'

'Why?' she demanded faintly. 'Why have you done this?'

'Your father needed help. He asked me for help.'

She was confused. 'You mean more help after the sale of the ponies?'

'You must have known that buying his stock would only temporarily bail him out of trouble. He needed more. The bank needed more.'

'So what are you saying?' She shook her head as if none of this made sense.

'I'm saying I bought the farm, paid off your father's debts and cleared his overdraft at the bank. He's a wealthy man now, so he can breed and train ponies to his heart's content. That's what he's good at, Jess. It's what he should be allowed to do. Business isn't his thing. And you need a life too.'

She frowned. 'And you decided this?'

'It was the best way to help your father and help you too.'

'Help yourself, don't you mean?' she flared. 'My father owns the best pasture in Yorkshire, the best gallops, the best ponies—or he will once the new foals are born and brought on. Anyone would want to buy Bell Farm.'

'Then why haven't they?' Dante asked bluntly. Jess blanched as he went on, 'According to your father, there hasn't been a single offer. He explained that not everyone has the appetite to live up here and cope with the climate and unrelenting work involved.'

'So what will be his position?' she demanded. 'Lackey to you?'

'He will do the job that suits him best, leaving my professional team to handle the business side of things. It's time to face facts. Your father needs more help than you can give him. You can't go on like this, working on the farm, caring for your father, maintaining a practice—

you're running yourself ragged. And you would still have the bank hounding you.'

'It's not up to you to decide how I handle this, or what I need,' she gritted out, filled with fury that any and all decisions had been made, irrespective of her opinion.

'So you don't want this?' Dante held out the document.

She waited for the red mist to clear before trusting herself to speak. What he said made a certain amount of sense. It was the way Dante was looking at her now that chilled her. So many people must have seen that same stare—in Dante's office, his boardroom or in his lawyer's office. It was a cool and decisive look that contained no emotion. Dante had struck a deal and that was that. Even half an hour ago she would have said it was impossible for him to treat her like this.

'It's a done deal,' he said as if to confirm her thoughts. 'It's what your father wanted, so there's no going back. You might as well accept—'

'I don't have to accept anything,' she interrupted. 'And I'm not prepared to say anything more to you until I've spoken to my father.'

'Be my guest,' Dante invited, glancing at the phone. 'I'll leave you to it,' he added, standing up. 'But I can assure you that your father is extremely happy with our deal. He sees it as a great way forward—for both of you.'

'So the two of you have decided my future without discussing it with me?'

'Your father didn't want to give you anything more

to worry about. He wanted to present it to you as a *fait accompli*. It's his farm to sell, Jess. He thought you'd be pleased. His knowledge and experience is invaluable to me, and now he'll have a wider role as advisor to all my equine facilities.'

'I can't deal with this right now.' She held up her hands, palms flat. 'I can't believe you've done this. I trusted you.'

'I'm not the enemy here, Jess.'

How could she deny her father what would be the most wonderful opportunity? She couldn't. She loved him too much. Protecting him was her mother's last wish, and this was a chance beyond their wildest dreams. But there was one thing she could refuse. 'You can take that contract with you. I don't want the farm. I haven't earned it.'

'You don't want your family farm, free from debt and with money in the bank?' Dante asked, frowning.

'If you're such a philanthropist, why didn't you give the farm to my father?'

'Because this was what he wanted, what he asked for. And this is what I want to do for you.'

'Seriously?' Jess shook her head. 'How do you think that makes me feel? Will you call by each time you're in Yorkshire to accept payment in kind?'

'*Dios*, Jess! Is that how little you think of me?'

'I don't know what to think,' she admitted, grabbing her coat. 'I'll speak to my father face to face, and then I'll decide what to do.'

CHAPTER SIXTEEN

It took Jess a while to catch her breath as she rushed down the lane leading home. Dante's offer was too much to take in. *He* was too much. She should have known better than to give way to feelings that had been ten long years in the making. Dante wanted more than she could give.

Huge sums of money passed through his hands on a regular basis, but his offer of the farm was incredible to Jess. It didn't seem right. She had to hear directly from her father that it was his wish too. Maybe he'd been blinded by the fact that Dante's offer put him back on top and hadn't thought things through.

She would do anything not to spoil his chances, but pride alone would stop her accepting Dante's gift. In monetary terms, she accepted that it was probably equal to Jess shaking out a few coins from her piggy bank, but that didn't make it right.

What made Dante's offer sting the most was that all she wanted was him, but Dante hadn't put that on the table. That wasn't part of his deal.

Jess marched towards the farmhouse entrance before suddenly hesitating. It was Christmas morning. Was she really going to ruin it with a blazing row with her father? Was that really what she wanted after all they'd been through? Changing course, she headed for the stables, made for it like a homing pigeon flying back to its roost. She had some serious thinking to do.

Diplomacy had never been his strong point, but he would not allow things between him and Jess to end like this. Tugging on his jacket, he headed out. It was a straight road to the farm and the directions were imprinted on his memory. He guessed he'd find Jess in the stable with the animals, where their company would warm her better than any brazier.

As he had expected, he found her hunched up in the bleak grey light on a hay bale. 'Hey…'

'Dante!' Jess didn't appear to breathe, and then noisily dragged in a huge gulp of air. 'I told you I needed time to think. Don't do this. You stunned me. I need space.'

'I'm here to make sure you got home safely.'

'I do know the way.'

'It can still be dangerous in this weather.'

'You're concerned about me now?' she challenged with a sceptical sideways look.

'Always.'

'Then why drop the bombshell about the farm as you did? Why cut me out of the discussions in the first place?'

'I could have led up to telling you with more grace,' he conceded, 'but I was impatient for you to know. As for cutting you out? I did what your father asked, but keeping you in the dark didn't sit well with me—hence my impatience to make things right.'

'It's all a mix-up,' she flared with a shake of her head. 'The only thing not in doubt is that you're an impatient man. Leaving hospital too soon. Riding before you could walk.'

He conceded all these comments with a shrug—all except one. 'I'm not always impatient. Not when it comes to you.'

She blushed at the reminder.

'You must see me as overbearing,' he confirmed with a shrug.

'You think?' she fired back.

'This was something I had to do for you, Jess.'

'I haven't had chance to speak to my father yet,' she admitted in an attempt to close the conversation down.

'What are you waiting for?' he challenged.

'You are overbearing, and you should have run this past me,' she stated hotly, 'but I won't disturb my father when he might have a second shot at happiness.'

'He's not here?'

'He's with Ella.'

He let that hang for a while and then remarked, 'It's good he's finally got his life back.'

'Meaning I haven't?' Jess suggested with an accusing look.

'You can do anything you choose to,' he said evenly. 'In the words of the cliché, the world is your oyster.'

'You mean, if I sell the farm back to you?'

'That's a novel idea.'

'I'm full of them.'

'I'd prefer you to keep the farm as your security going forward,' he said honestly. 'You don't have to live here. You can live anywhere you like.'

'Your people will move in to help out,' she intuited.

'If you want them to—they're waiting for your instructions.'

'You've thought of everything, haven't you, Dante?'

He remained silent.

Averting her face, Jess chewed her thumb before turning back to face him. 'This is all about trust,' she said.

'Without it we're going nowhere,' he agreed.

'*We?*' she queried.

There was a long silence, and then she said, 'Isn't time supposed to heal all wounds?'

'Some cut deeper than others and leave scars we have to deal with, but they do get better over time.'

She looked at him as if she wanted to believe him. 'I didn't mean to make this about me. I just wish I had my mother to confide in sometimes.'

'I understand that. It's as if we've both been set adrift. I was without an anchor for years until I got my head together and knew we must pull together as a family. You've changed and grown too,' he reminded Jess. 'You completed your training, as you promised your mother you would, and now you're an excellent physiotherapist. Here's the living proof,' he added with a flourish as he spread his hands wide.

'No cane,' Jess agreed with the glimmer of a smile. 'Your return to polo's been well documented, though playing like the devil on horseback so soon after your recovery is asking for trouble.'

He seized on her cue. 'That's why I need you. See what happens when you leave me to my own devices?'

'As I remember it, my contract ended and you appointed someone else in my place.'

'To take over your good work,' he pointed out.

'Yet now you risk that good work by launching yourself like an avenging angel on Nero Caracas and his team.'

'The important thing is, my team won.'

'Of course it did,' Jess agreed with the lift of a brow. 'And by some miracle you survived.'

'No miracle,' he argued. 'My recovery is thanks to extremely effective therapy from a certain Señorita Slatehome.' He didn't want to talk about that. He wanted to talk about Jess. She was all that mattered. He wanted her to trust him and relax in his company. He'd handled things badly when he told her about the farm, but his remorse was genuine and he wanted her to have security in the future, whatever choice she made next.

'Just don't take too many chances in the future,' she warned.

He shrugged. 'See what happens when you cut me loose? There's only one way to sort this. The next time I play polo you'd better be there.'

'What are you saying, Dante?'

'I'm admitting I need you,' he confessed.

'As a therapist?'

'What do you think?'

'I think it makes sense from that point of view to keep me on speed dial.'

'Speed dial?' His lips pressed down as he considered this for all of a split second. 'I'm not sure that would suit either of us.'

Even in the dim light he saw her blush at this reminder of their inexhaustible appetite for each other.

'Will you be heading home now?' she asked on the way to recovering her composure.

'Not until I know you've spoken to your father, and I feel confident you're reassured about what's happening with the farm.'

Then he would leave, with or without Jess. If he'd been in doubt about the nature of love, he understood now that it sometimes involved sacrifice, and if staying here was what Jess wanted he had no option but to let her go. He had been overbearing with his purchase of her family's farm and in trying to help her father he'd only succeeded in railroading Jess. She couldn't fight him. The sale was a done deal, and she wouldn't do anything to upset her father's future.

'Dante—'

'Yes?' He hardly knew what to expect. Jess's face was tight with tension.

'I can't let you go without telling you I love you.'

Her eyes snapped shut after this statement. She didn't move. She didn't breathe and then, with a ragged exhalation of air, she opened her eyes and zoned in on his. 'I love you,' she repeated with fiery emphasis.

His entire body thrilled. Jess's words were a statement, a challenge, a baring of her soul that rang in his head like a carillon of happy Christmas bells.

'I'm not going anywhere.' Closing the distance between them in a couple of strides, he lifted Jess into his arms. Sacrifice was one thing, but he was the kind of man who always had to fight tooth and nail for what he believed in. He should have known that all along.

Urgency consumed them both. Jess met him with matching fire. She was already reaching for him. They didn't trouble to undress completely. Just enough to fall back on the hay and mate like wild animals. It was a wordless, mindless coupling that said everything about how far they'd come, and how deep was their trust.

'It feels as if we've come full circle,' Jess murmured as they put their clothes back in order.

'This is where we first met,' he agreed with a grin. 'And things get more interesting each time.'

'There's a new litter of kittens,' she warned, 'so watch out.'

She smiled. So did he, and as they stared into each other's eyes he knew the situation could be rescued, but lovemaking wasn't enough. He had to prove to Jess that when it came to business he might be brusque, brisk and to the point, but he hadn't meant to hurt her over the farm, as he so obviously had.

Stable cats and dogs stood by, ready to assist him. Jess's motley assortment of strays and beloved pets had sensed they were needed and had gathered around them to provide a welcome distraction. Neither Jess nor he could remain immune to them for long, or remain tense, not with animals around.

When she'd fed them some treats Jess held up her grimy fingernails and grimaced. 'I'll never make it in your world. I'm just too down-homey and—'

'Chilled out?' he suggested. 'Don't you think that's what I need?'

'Just as well,' she commented, grimacing as she took in the damage to her sweater from a new naughty kitten.

'I still love you,' he said as she pulled a face.

Her gaze flashed up to his. 'Please don't say that unless you mean it.'

'I love you,' he said again, his eye-line steady on Jess's.

'Don't make this any harder than it has to be,' she said firmly. 'especially when I know you're about to leave.'

He shrugged. 'What's so hard about leaving with me? Or are you more concerned about dealing with the damage from a leaking kitten?'

'Don't make a joke of this,' she said softly.

'Because…?'

'Because I love you too much for that.'

'Then be with me always.'

'Always? As in for ever?' she exclaimed, incredulous. 'As your therapist?'

'As my wife. I can't think of anyone else who'd have you,' he teased with a pointed look at the stain on Jess's sweater. 'Let me love you as you deserve. Let me spoil you. Let me lavish things on you.'

'You should know by now that's not me. I don't need any of those things.'

'But you'll grow to love being spoiled, I promise,' he insisted.

'I love *you*,' she stated firmly, 'not what you can give me.'

'As I love you,' he said, 'but you must allow me to have the pleasure of giving you things. Love, and gifts like the farm are not mutually exclusive, so get used to it because there's a lot more coming your way. The farm is just the beginning.'

'But I haven't given you my answer yet,' she pointed out.

'I'm not a patient man,' he warned.

'So I shouldn't push you too hard?' she suggested.

'Unless it's in bed.'

'Do you take anything seriously?' she scolded.

'I'm extremely serious when I take you.' And when she shook her head, he added, 'I love you for everything you are, and everything you will be in the future. So what's your answer?'

Jess gasped as he dragged her close. 'My answer's yes. I'll come with you wherever you go.'

'You can depend on it,' he promised.

A few potent seconds ticked by while they laughed and took in the trust that was the bedrock of their decision to be together for ever, but then, as might have been expected, their control snapped at exactly the same moment and as Jess reached for him he drove his mouth down on hers.

It was a long time later when Jess fell back, exhausted. They could never get enough of each other and had made love fiercely, tenderly and, last of all, and most affecting of all, they had made love slowly and deliberately, with love and trust in their eyes, while Dante told Jess she was the only woman he could ever love and that he would be proud to have her at his side for the rest of his life.

'There's so much we don't know about each other,' she whispered, frowning as she turned languidly in his arms.

'Great,' Dante approved. 'So much to learn about each other. New surprises each day.'

She had to be certain. 'Are you sure I'm enough for you? I'm not fancy. I live a plain life in plain clothes, surrounded by plain-speaking people.'

'Enough for me?' he exclaimed softly. 'You're perfect for me. And to prove I'm serious I've got something for you.'

'Nothing expensive, I hope?' Laughter pealed out of her as Dante produced a wisp of hay.

'Jessica Slatehome, sometimes known as Skylar… I'm prepared to be adaptable when it comes to you, so I'm asking again, formally this time, will you marry me?'

'You know my answer, but I'll happily give it again *formally*,' she teased, knowing her face must betray her feelings. 'My answer's yes.'

'Now, I've just got to get this to stay on,' Dante said, frowning as he secured the hay ring around her marriage finger with a few well-judged twists.

Jess stared at her hay ring. She loved it as much as any diamond a fashionable jeweller.

'This is just a start,' Dante insisted, 'We can't change who we are, and it would be wrong to try and change each other.'

'But how will I fit in to your glamorous life?'

'You'll fit in perfectly. We fit together perfectly,' he added, though as he'd moved over her to prove his point, Jess kept her opinion to herself. Providing therapy for injured athletes was her life's work. Riding the horses she loved was her passion. That was the world where she belonged.

Was it? Was it really?

How could she live without Dante? How would she feel if she saw him with other women, knowing she hadn't even put up a fight for the best thing in her life? Were her dreams dust? Was it even possible to hold on to her familiar world while sharing his? 'You're at the top of your field in the tech world, and on the polo circuit,' she mused when they were quiet again. 'And although I could happily fit into your equine world, I belong backstage, not out front with the beautiful people.'

'Is that a fact?' Dante queried with a long sideways look as he set about repeating what he did so very well.

'In my opinion,' he added much much later, 'you outshine anyone I've ever met. When men on the polo circuit are as dazzled by your beauty as I am I'll have to flatten them. Is that good enough for you? There's no question of you being backstage. You'll be at my side and for ever, I hope.'

'Dante—'

'What?'

She gave a long sigh of pleasure.

'I hear you,' he reassured as he brushed her mouth with lingering kisses. 'You don't want to talk now. You want this, you need this, so please don't ever stop?'

'For ever is a long time,' she reminded him in between hectic gasps of breath.

Dante shrugged as he moved firmly towards the inevitable conclusion. 'That's one thing over which we'll have to agree to disagree. For ever with you can never be long enough for me. Merry Christmas, Jess.'

CHAPTER SEVENTEEN

MORE THAN A week later, when Jess had spent quality time with her father and Dante had spent earthy, intimate, getting to know her every which-way time with Jess, they boarded his private jet to return to Spain. He was happy to think Jess was doubly reassured—not just by the news that the arrangement for the farm suited her father, but by something even better than that.

'It's never too late to fall in love,' Jim Slatehome had explained to both of them, saying he'd been struck by lightning when he had the opportunity to get to know his neighbour Ella again.

Confident that her father was not only financially secure but was happy and well looked after, Jess was ready to embark on her new life. Everyone, including the animals, was on tenterhooks at the thought of her return to what Maria described as Jess's home.

Dante owned numerous properties across the world. Jess could take her pick. He imagined she might choose his simple shack on a Pacific island, judging by the way she'd held on to the wisp of hay he'd tied around her wedding finger.

That was Jess. That was the Jess he loved. The

woman who had insisted she needed no other ring. He'd taken her at her word. For now.

It had taken him a short time or a little over ten years, depending on how he looked at it, to win Jess's trust and now she could have whatever she wanted. Nothing could corrupt her moral compass and, with their lives ahead of them, she'd have plenty of opportunity to counter his riches with hay bales and sound common sense. They were like two pieces of a jigsaw that fitted together perfectly and he could never repay her for what she'd given him.

They'd slept at the pub each night after Christmas, and each night before she slept he told Jess how much he loved her, and how much he owed her, not just for healing him but for teaching him how to trust, and to give his heart deeply and completely. Those quiet times alone had allowed him to reassure her that she would never have to give up her career. His proposal was that Jess headed up a travelling clinic, so they could be together wherever he played polo. She had instantly approved the idea and was excited to make a start. He was confident she'd soon build up a regular practice, especially with him around as visible proof of Jess's excellence as a therapist.

She was playing with the hay wisp, he noticed, turning it round and round her finger. 'I can't believe you managed to hold on to that,' he admitted. 'You can have a ring of your choice as soon as we land in Spain. You can design your own, if you like.'

She gave him a teasing smile. 'It would have to look exactly like this one.'

'I'm sure that can be arranged.'

She remained silent for a while and then she said, 'Could we have a Christmas wedding?'

'You can have a wedding whenever and wherever you like. We don't have to get married at all.'

'Is that your get-out?' she half scolded, half teased him. 'Are you tired of me already?'

'I will never tire of you.' His heart had found its home and wanted no other.

'Then next Christmas it is,' she declared happily, clearly brim-full of excitement. 'There's something special about the holiday season, don't you think?'

'It won't be snowing in Spain,' he cautioned.

'Not where you live,' she agreed.

He thought of his ski chalet, high in the Sierra Nevada, and conceded, 'Snow can be arranged.'

Jess laughed. 'Is there anything you can't do?'

He huffed a sigh as he thought about this for the time it took to kiss her neck and then her lips. 'Resist you?' he suggested. 'But remember, if you're set on this idea of a Christmas wedding, there's almost a year to wait.'

'For the veil and the dress,' she pointed out.

He laughed as he got the picture. 'You are a shameless hussy.'

'You made me so.'

'I plead innocent,' he fired back with amusement. 'It must have been Skylar who led me astray.'

'Can she do so again?' Jess suggested as the aircraft levelled off.

'There are several bedrooms in the back—take your pick.'

'Lead the way,' she whispered.

A little less than one year later

Christmas Day was approaching fast. Since moving to Spain to live on Dante's *estancia*, Jess had travelled the world. Watching Dante play polo and dispensing necessary therapy, both to his polo-playing associates and to Dante under rather more intimate circumstances, had given her a new insight into the lives of the super-rich.

They had the same worries and the same ailments as everyone else, but some were so remote and removed from the realities of everyday life she felt sorry for them. Rather than envy their so-called gilded existence, she thought of them, locked in their ivory towers with their sights set on some far-off horizon, missing the little things down on the ground that, in Jess's opinion, made life worth living.

Dante's sister Sofia was a glaring exception. They thought alike, and Sofia had become Jess closest friend. Sofia had persuaded Jess that she could navigate the role of star player's wife, and billionaire's soulmate, with the same grace with which Jess handled her job at the mobile clinic. 'You love him. That's all that matters,' Sofia had pointed out. 'And my brother adores you. I love you because you brought him back to us. I've never seen Dante like this before. He wants to be with his family. He wants to share us with you. You've healed him in more ways than one.'

Both Jess and Sofia were excited that Maria and her relatives had agreed to play a major role in Jess's wedding ceremony, providing music and dance. Jess wanted a real party and for everyone to join in. As

Dante had promised, their marriage would be celebrated high on the Sierra Nevada mountain range, where snow and fiery passion went hand in hand.

Sofia's wedding gift for Jess couldn't have pleased her more. It was a new horse blanket for Moon. The mare had fretted for Jess, Dante had explained, and so the pony she'd loved since the day Moon was born was his wedding gift to Jess.

Sofia had insisted on giving Jess a few more small presents—or 'thingamajigs' as Sofia liked to call them.

'I want to spoil you with bits of nonsense,' she'd said.

'Not nonsense,' Jess had protested as she opened the boxes of accessories—hairbands, bracelets that jingled and Spanish mantilla combs with filmy, lacy veils. 'These are lovely, thoughtful gifts.'

She only wished Sofia could find the same happiness she had.

'Here comes the groom. He's going to be late,' Sofia announced tensely.

Looking out of the window, Jess saw Dante and his brothers skiing up to the door of his magnificent chalet. Her heart sang at the sight of Dante, as skilful on snow as he was on Zeus, his mighty black stallion. He had to do something first thing in the morning, Dante had told her last night, or he wouldn't be capable of staying away from his bride before their wedding.

The year leading up to this moment had been packed full of polo and patients and horses and Dante, which was pretty much everything Jess could ask of life. Dante hadn't forced the issue when he asked her to marry him and, predictably, that had made her want him all the more. The ring she would wear when they were married remained the only bone of contention between them.

'A plain gold band will do me,' she'd insisted, while Dante had countered by assuring her that the first time they made love as man and wife Jess would be wearing nothing but diamonds.

'The first time?' Jess had queried with amusement.

'The first time as husband and wife,' Dante had countered before taking her in the most delicious way.

Would she ever get enough of him? Not a chance, Jess concluded as she watched him shoulder his skis. There was a sense of purpose and a particular speed to his actions she recognised. Dante wouldn't be late for his wedding, because he was already thinking about taking her to bed.

'Jess? Your gown,' Sofia prompted.

Jess turned to see the sparkling lace and chiffon dream of a dress Dante had insisted must come from Paris. It was a restrained and beautiful creation, a fairy tale dress, as Sofia described it, and one that made dreams come true.

Arranging the gown reverently on the bed, Sofia stood back. 'I can't wait to have you as a sister,' she admitted, glowing with pent-up excitement.

'I'm already your sister,' Jess insisted as they exchanged the warmest of hugs. 'Skylar too?' Sofia teased as they broke apart.

'Of course. We can't leave her out, can we?'

'And now this dream of a dress,' Sofia said as she lifted it carefully from the bed.

Jess had dreamed of this moment since that first encounter with Dante in her father's stable ten years ago and now, quite incredibly, those dreams were about to come true.

'Not incredible,' Sofia argued when Jess voiced these thoughts. 'My brother is lucky to have found you. A woman less likely to be cast about by the winds of fate, I have yet to meet. You are a strong, determined woman who will bloom wherever you're planted, and I'm proud to be your friend.'

Jess was so popular on the *estancia* everyone had made a special effort to travel to the mountains to attend her wedding ceremony, which was as relaxed and authentic as Jess had always dreamed it would be. to make things easier for their guests, Dante had laid on two of his aircraft to bring them in from far and wide. Sofia had dipped into her billions too, to ensure the most magical scene.

A huge pavilion had been erected in the deep snow in the garden of Dante's chalet overlooking the dramatic mountain range. Fairy lights were strung lavishly around, while a pathway of pink rose petals, edged by sweet-smelling country flowers flown in from Yorkshire, filled the air with delicate scent. The ambient temperature inside the pavilion was cosy, thanks to heaters hidden in the roof, and the guests agreed they had never been more comfortable at a wedding than they were on the deeply upholstered white seats. Haunting music from a single acoustic guitar set the romantic mood, while candles glowed on the altar and jewel-coloured lanterns cast a magical glow across the excited congregation.

Peeping through the entrance, Jess saw her father seated with Ella on the front row. They looked so happy together and, never one to miss a business trick, her father had flown in from England on one of Dante's specially adapted jets accompanied by not just his lively and down-to-earth partner but by several promising ponies as well.

There was a Christmas tree in the entrance covered with small gifts for their guests. Dante had told Jess that her gift was the small brown paper-covered box at the top of the tree and that she must claim it and open it before she came down the aisle.

One of the taller attendants got it down for her, and when she opened it she gasped. It was a perfect replica of Jess's hay twist ring, but crafted in pure rose gold.

Her wedding ring was perfect and so was the groom, Jess thought when Dante turned at the moment she appeared and their eyes met.

Every seat was taken by Dante's family and staff, and by a select number of guests. Maria had settled into the chalet weeks ago to prepare food and the mix of delicious cooking smells had stayed with him, making him hungry, and hungry for Jess. *Dios*, where was she? When could they get away from here?

At last!

His heart filled with love as he caught sight of his bride, who looked beyond ravishingly beautiful as she walked up the petal-strewn aisle.

'Thank you for my ring,' Jess whispered when she reached his side. 'It's absolutely perfect. I have something for you...'

'What?' he demanded as Jess turned to hand over her bouquet to Sofia, thinking of all the small, thoughtful gifts Jess had bought him in the lead up to the wedding. Her answer was to take hold of his hand and rest it gently against her stomach. A lightning bolt of excitement struck him as Jess stared up with eyes full of trust.

'You…?' He was stunned into silence, and not just because the celebrant had indicated that the ceremony was about to begin.

'Yes,' Jess confirmed. 'We're having a baby. We're going to be adding to the Acosta clan soon.'

'Oh, *Dios*!' he exclaimed on a hectic rush of breath. 'Thank you! Thank you!'

'You may *not* yet kiss your bride,' the priest scolded them with a twinkle in his eyes.

But Dante Acosta had always broken the rules, as had Skylar, so they kissed passionately and everyone applauded until at last, with love surrounding them on every side, Jess and Dante were married.

* * * * *

Adored One Scandalous Christmas Eve?
Why not explore these other Susan Stephens stories?

A Scandalous Midnight in Madrid
The Greek's Virgin Temptation
Snowbound with His Forbidden Innocent
A Bride Fit for a Prince?

Available now!

WE HOPE YOU ENJOYED
THIS BOOK FROM
⊕ HARLEQUIN
PRESENTS

Escape to exotic locations where passion knows no bounds.

Welcome to the glamorous lives of royals and billionaires, where passion knows no bounds. Be swept into a world of luxury, wealth and exotic locations.

8 NEW BOOKS AVAILABLE EVERY MONTH!

#3861 THE RULES OF HIS BABY BARGAIN
by Louise Fuller
Casino mogul Charlie Law promised his dying father he'd find his infant half brother and bring him home. He didn't allow for the baby's aunt and guardian, beautiful Dora Thorn, to counter his every move!

#3862 INNOCENT IN THE SHEIKH'S PALACE
by Dani Collins
Plain librarian Hannah Meeks decided to start the family she's desperately wanted—on her own. Only to discover that her miracle baby is actually the heir to Sheikh Akin Sarraf's desert throne...

#3863 PLAYING THE BILLIONAIRE'S GAME
by Pippa Roscoe
Fourteen days. That's how long exiled Duke Sebastian gives art valuer Sia Keating to prove he stole a famous painting. And how long she'll have to avoid the pull of embracing their dangerous attraction...

#3864 THE VOWS HE MUST KEEP
The Avelar Family Scandals
by Amanda Cinelli
Tycoon Valerio Marchesi swore to keep Daniela Avelar safe. Discovering she's in grave danger, he insists she becomes his bride! But their engagement of convenience is a red-hot fire burning out of control!

HPCNMRB1020

The hottest actor in Bollywood, Vikram Raawal has found love countless times—on-screen. In real life, he's given up on finding a soul-deep connection. Until at a masquerade ball, shy assistant Naina Menon leaves him craving more…

Read on for a sneak preview of Tara Pammi's next story for Harlequin Presents, Claiming His Bollywood Cinderella.

The scent of her hit him first. A subtle blend of jasmine and that he'd remember for the rest of his life. And equate with honesty and irreverence and passion and laughter. There was a joy about this woman, despite her insecurities and vulnerabilities, that he found almost magical.

The mask she wore was black satin with elaborate gold threading at the edges and was woven tightly into her hair, leaving just enough of her beautiful dark brown eyes visible. The bridge of her small nose was revealed as was the slice of her cheekbones. For a few seconds, Vikram had the overwhelming urge to tear it off. He wanted to see her face. Not because he wanted to find out her identity.

He wanted to see her face because he wanted to know this woman. He wanted to know everything about her. He wanted… With a rueful shake of his head, he pushed away the urge. It was more than clear that men had only ever disappointed her. He was damned if he was going to be counted as one of them. He wanted to be different in her memory.

When she remembered him after tonight, he wanted her to smile. He wanted her to crave more of him. Just as he would crave more of her. He knew this before their lips even touched. And he would find a way to discover her identity. He was just as sure of that, too.

Her mouth was completely uncovered. Her lipstick was mostly gone, leaving a faint pink smudge that he wanted to lick away with his tongue.

She held the edge of her silk dress with one hand, and as she lifted it to move, he got a flash of a thigh. Soft and smooth and silky. It was like receiving a jolt of electricity with every inch he discovered of this woman. The dress swooped low in the front, baring the upper curves of her breasts in a tantalizing display.

And then there she was, within touching distance. Sitting with her legs folded beneath her, looking straight into his eyes. One arm held the sofa while the other smoothed repeatedly over the slight curve of her belly. She was nervous and he found it both endearing and incredibly arousing. She wanted to please herself. And him. And he'd never wanted more for a woman to discover pleasure with him.

Her warm breath hit him somewhere between his mouth and jaw in silky strokes that resonated with his heartbeat. This close, he could see the tiny scar on the other corner of her mouth.

"Are you going to do anything?" she asked after a couple of seconds, sounding completely put out.

He wanted to laugh and tug that pouty lower lip with his teeth. Instead he forced himself to take a breath. He was never going to smell jasmine and not think of her ever again. "It's your kiss, darling. You take it."

Don't miss
Claiming His Bollywood Cinderella,
available November 2020 wherever
Harlequin Presents books and ebooks are sold.

Harlequin.com

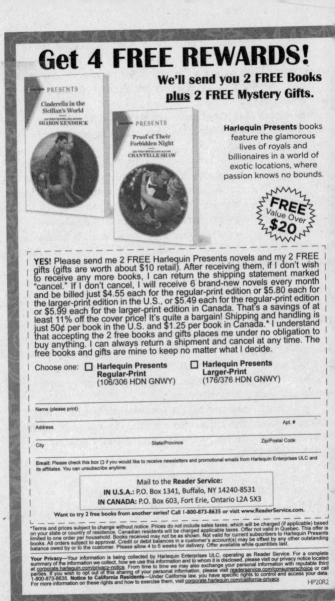